"I'm not ta[barcode D0485803]**ght now, Jana.**

Witt tapped her head, making her look up at him. She knew she'd be lost when she did, for the look in his eyes seemed to go right through her. There wasn't any hope of hiding what had grown between them at that point. Whether it made business sense or not hardly mattered. "I'm talking as your…friend," he said, the hesitation speaking volumes. After a moment, he leaned in and left a soft kiss on her cheek. She felt herself dissolve under the tenderness. "As someone who…cares about you."

She didn't even realize that her hand had lifted to the spot where he'd kissed her until she followed his gaze. "Witt…"

"Yeah," he said softly, touching her hand as it lay against her cheek. "We're going to have to figure out what to do about that. But not now."

Allie Pleiter, an award-winning author and RITA® Award finalist, writes both fiction and nonfiction. Her passion for knitting shows up in many of her books and all over her life. Entirely too fond of French macarons and lemon meringue pie, Allie spends her days writing books and avoiding housework. Allie grew up in Connecticut, holds a BS in speech from Northwestern University and lives near Chicago, Illinois.

Visit the Author Profile page at Harlequin.com for more titles.

The Texan's
Second Chance

Allie Pleiter

HARLEQUIN® LOVE INSPIRED®

Recycling programs
for this product may
not exist in your area.

LOVE INSPIRED BOOKS

ISBN-13: 978-0-373-81925-6

The Texan's Second Chance

"For I know the plans I have for you," declares the Lord, "plans to prosper you and not to harm you, plans to give you hope and a future."

—*Jeremiah* 29:11

To Elizabeth
Because great partnerships
truly are hard to come by

Chapter One

Jana Powers stared at the truck in front of her. "It's blue."

Her new boss, Witt Buckton, didn't seem to especially mind. "Yes, it is."

Jana pushed up her sleeves. She'd tried to dress professionally for this first meeting with her supervisor, wearing her chef's coat, but even in October Austin was still too warm for it. Texas could still hit ninety degrees on a daily basis in the fall. "No, I mean it's *really* blue." The food truck was, in fact, an alarmingly bright turquoise. Brilliantly blue. One might accurately say "loud." Uh-oh. Was Witt Buckton one of "those" kinds of restaurant owners—the kind who put public relations above everything and cared more about gimmicks than quality?

Keep an open mind. Ellie said this guy was

smart and nice. Then again, this guy was Ellie's cousin, and Ellie was really more colleague than friend.

She stared at the vividly hued truck again. From a marketing standpoint, the color might make sense—it certainly stood out, and was memorable—but who would want to eat in a glow that intense? She might have to don sunglasses just to work inside the thing. *Please, don't let it be that color on the inside.*

"It's a marketing thing." Jana was glad to note a touch of apology in Witt's voice that hinted maybe his priorities weren't totally skewed toward PR. "The color is a trademark for the Blue Thorn Ranch."

Jana looked at him. He was part of the Buckton family—the clan who had owned the Blue Thorn Ranch for several generations and to which her former coworker Ellie belonged—but he was a cousin, not one of the immediate family. Still, a long look allowed her to connect the dots almost instantly. Ellie was a Buckton, and her eyes were the same brilliant turquoise as Witt's. If those eyes were a family trait, then she could understand why the ranch had adopted that shade as its trademark. "I get it," she offered. "But—" here she applied her friendliest smile "—don't you think you went a bit overboard on the paint job?"

Oops. Witt's eyes went a touch cold, and Jana fought the urge to whack her own forehead. *Not everyone needs to hear every opinion you've got. Especially not your new boss. Remember how much you want this job?*

"I told you to meet me at the blue truck," Witt said in a crisp, mildly annoyed tone. He tucked his hands in his pockets. "Tell me, did you have any trouble finding the blue truck?"

He had her there—she saw it from three blocks away. "No."

"My point exactly. To patronize a food truck—a mobile enterprise by definition—you have to be able to find it, don't you?

Jana swallowed her distaste for people who used business buzzwords like *enterprise.*

"True, but a color never sold a hamburger or a steak sandwich. *Food* is what attracts customers. Good, quality food." Good, quality food was what Jana did best. Let all the fancy chefs have their fusion cuisines and trendy menus. Jana's passion—why God put her on the earth, as far as she was concerned—was comfort food. The ordinary, memory-laden food people turned to when a day had gone bad or a boyfriend had split or life had kicked them in the teeth some other way. Supposedly, that was why the Bucktons had hired her. If it wasn't, best to settle that right now. "You're not expecting adventure-burgers out of me, are you?"

That popped his turquoise eyes wide. "Adventure-burgers?"

Jana started walking toward the truck, eager to confirm that her new workspace wasn't screaming blue on the inside as well as the outside. "You know what I mean. Bison ranches like the Blue Thorn are pretty unusual, which means the bison meat from the ranch is unique enough on its own. I'm not going to invent crazy toppings or obscure ingredients just to draw attention. That's not what I do."

"And that's not what we want," Witt assured her. "Blue Thorn produces high-quality, delicious meat that we want to share with the community by way of this food truck. Nobody wants you to hide it under Ugandan spotted goat curd or anything like that."

She eyed him, surprised he could name an ingredient she'd never heard of.

"Okay, I made that one up," he admitted. "But you get the point." He produced a set of keys from his pocket and unlocked the back of the truck. Jana bit back a comment about the vehicle being even brighter at close range. *I won't need coffee to wake up—I'll just stare at this for thirty seconds,* she mused to herself. She braced herself as her new boss pulled open the doors…

To reveal a blessedly white interior, brand spanking new and immaculately clean. "Wow," Jana gasped involuntarily, struck—in the best possible way—by the perfectness of it all. Her own kitchen. It didn't matter one bit that it was small, mobile and wrapped in a neon aqua paint job. This would be *her* kitchen, where she finally got to call the shots. A fresh start she very much needed. The thrill of it sparkled all the way out to Jana's fingertips as she touched the gleaming counter.

"Ellie made sure the basics were here, but we're going to go to the restaurant supply place this afternoon so you can pick out whatever else you need."

Free rein in the restaurant supply store? Jana could think of few things that would make her happier. "Absolutely fine by me." Her hand went involuntarily to the messenger bag at her side, which not only held the usual purse contents, but her chef's knife set—the pride, joy and personal treasure of anyone who cooked for a living. The knives seemed ready to climb out of her bag and spread themselves on the counter. She looked back at Witt, hoping the eagerness thumping in her chest showed in her eyes to make up for her earlier crack about the color. "You're off to a good start. This is a really good setup."

"I thought so." Witt pulled open the refrigerator under the back counter to reveal several packets wrapped in brown paper. "Today we'll get to try her out. I want to be the one to eat the first burger made in this truck."

The demand bugged her. Did he expect her to audition for a job she already had? "I have cooked for Ellie and Gunner, you know." Surely he knew Ellie's brother Gunner—the current owner of the Blue Thorn Ranch, and the one who had made the decision a few years ago to switch the ranch from cattle to bison—had approved her as chef two weeks ago. Witt had been called out of town that night, which was why today was the first day she met her new immediate boss.

Witt walked around the truck, opening empty cabinets and drawers. "I know, and I'm sorry I missed that. There's no question you're already hired. This is more of an…indulgence." His face tightened just the slightest bit. "You don't have to do a ton of stuff to the kitchen before you can cook in it, right?"

As confident as he'd been before, defending the decision to paint the truck blue, that's how uncertain he sounded now. He really didn't have a clue about what was involved in running a kitchen, did he? Jana had worked for too many restaurant owners who thought they knew everything about cooking but were really only checkbooks. Lots of owners pretended at expertise and talent, getting in the way of good cooking when all they really needed to do was to play host. Management had its place, but so did cooking. Right now Jana still wasn't sure Witt Buckton recognized the difference.

You don't want to go back to Atlanta. Make this work. Jana pulled her knife kit from her bag and set it on the counter, the act feeling like a blessing of the space. "I won't need too much at first."

"You don't think it's weird that I want to give the truck a private inauguration?" His face softened from its "I'm in charge" expression that had dug under her skin. Now it showed just a bit of the anxiety she was already fighting.

He's not like Ronnie. This business seemed to have heart, and heart was what Jana loved most in cooking. Maybe this gig wouldn't be bad after all. "Nah. I think I'd do the same thing."

"You will, technically. You didn't think I

was going to make you just sit there and feed me, did you?"

Actually, that's exactly what she'd assumed.

"No," he corrected, "We're going to eat a meal together, you and I."

Jana had to admit, she liked what his eyes did when he said that. He wasn't wearing a suit—quite the contrary, Witt Buckton wore brown jeans and a light blue chambray shirt that did un-boss-like things to his eyes. His shirt was crisply ironed, but his jeans and boots were more down-home than corner office.

"Oh, wait," he said as he reached into one of the upper cabinets and pulled out a package. "This first. Ellie said you ought to have one of these, and it couldn't be just any old one."

Jana pulled open the package he handed to her. What unfolded out of the wrappings was the nicest, most stylish chef's coat Jana had ever seen. Made of a mercifully light fabric—perfect for the hot, tight confines of a food truck—the coat had three-quarter-length sleeves with a clever row of off-center buttons. Turquoise piping, shoulder panels, buttons and collar gave it just enough of what she now interpreted as the Blue Thorn signature color.

Best of all, the coat wasn't the usual boxy cut, but fitted to a woman's physique. It was, by all accounts, pretty. Feminine, yet serious, right down to the "Chef Jana" embroidered above the stylized "BT" that was the Blue Thorn logo.

"It's fabulous," she exclaimed, meaning it. "Really, you have no idea. Some of these things can be real sacks. I was expecting an apron or something, but this…" She touched it again, a little bit stunned. She hadn't expected anything like this, especially from a setup as small as Blue Thorn seemed to be. "Wow."

"Why would you expect an apron? Chefs don't wear aprons. Chefs wear coats. You're not just any old food server, Jana. You're going to be the force behind Blue Thorn Burgers. You will be the only face most people ever associate with everything we're trying to do."

Jana had learned to be suspicious of guys who laid it on quite so thick. Still, it was better than being dismissed as just the hands holding the spatula. "I'm up for it. I'll build you a following so loyal you'll have to start buses running out to the ranch for tours."

He laughed. "Ellie would probably love that. Gunner, not so much." Witt had a nice laugh that made her laugh, as well. "By the way, Ellie said she will deck you out in knitted scarves, hats and fingerless mitts—whatever those are—to match if the weather gets too chilly in here."

Hardly a surprise there—Ellie was known for her love of knitting. She'd even turned her hobby into a new career. When they'd first met, Ellie had been working in marketing for a restaurant chain in Atlanta, but it was well-known that she always had a knitting project in her bag. Now that she was settled back in Texas, she worked part time for the Austin Restaurateurs Association, and she also ran a newly developed yarn business for the ranch, branding and marketing knitting yarn made out of bison hair.

Witt fiddled with a stove knob. "Can't really picture it getting cold enough to need a scarf in here. We're more likely to have the opposite problem. It's a good thing we've got almost a year to learn how to cope with how this place will swelter starting in May. What do you say we fire up the engine so we can turn on the air-conditioning?" Buckton held up the keys—on a little buffalo-shaped key chain, no less. "You got your commercial license so you're cleared to drive this, right?"

Jana stowed her bag in a little compartment behind the driver's seat and slipped behind the wheel. "Yes, Ellie told me to take care of that as soon as I moved here." She looked at her boss. "How'd *you* get it here?"

He grinned. "I got a commercial license, too. I figured it was best if we had at least one person from the company brass who could drive this thing."

So this "company brass" wasn't afraid to get hands-on. She remembered Ellie saying his branch of the family were ranchers as well, so maybe that wasn't so hard to believe.

Jana twisted the key in the ignition, the truck chugging to life with a solid sound. The wheel felt satisfying in her hands. From inside, she could almost forget the truck's circus color and feel powerful at the helm. She noticed—gladly—that he hadn't insisted on driving. *When will you stop thinking all men behave the way Ronnie did?* "I take it we're going to Allen?" she called over her shoulder. The southern part of Austin had one of the best restaurant supply shops in the area. Anyone who cared enough to get that sharp a chef's coat knew enough to be shopping at Allen Restaurant Supply. She'd been known to pore over their website for entertainment.

"Where else?"

Jana smiled, feeling the warmth of it spread right down her throat like a cup of the most excellent coffee on a chilly morning. "Well, then, let's go shopping."

What were you expecting?

Witt stared at the feisty brunette behind the wheel. Whatever he'd been expecting, Jana Powers wasn't it. She was…feminine. He felt ashamed that his cowboy sensibilities had imagined that a burger-food-truck chef ought to be a bit rougher around the edges, and generally much less…what? He couldn't produce the correct adjective, and maybe that was for the best. Witt got the distinct impression that voicing the thoughts currently buzzing in his head might earn him a swift kick in the shins from his new chef. Jana was what Gran would most definitely call a spitfire.

Jana was different, all right. Would that be good? Would the burger crowd—something he considered a decidedly male customer base—go for someone like her? *Why not? Guys like burgers. Guys like girls. A girl— a woman—who could cook a great burger?* He couldn't have planned a better public relations platform if he'd tried.

In the restaurant supply store, Jana came positively alive with energy and purpose. "These," she said, hoisting up a pair of frying pans with such a look of triumph that it was as if they were gold-medal trophies, "are the ones we need. They cost a bit more, but they're worth it." He could tell it was a test—would he spring for the good stuff or cut corners?

He nodded. "If that's what you need."

"You want simple food exquisitely done, right?"

He chose her term. "You got it. No adventure-burgers."

Jana's face broke into an electric smile. Honestly, she looked half kid in a candy store, half rock star spinning drumsticks as she gave the pair of pans a celebratory twirl before placing them in the cart he was pushing through the aisles. Her thick, curly brown hair bounced around her face as she selected implements, tubs of condiments and other supplies. Sure, he was watching funds fly out of the company checkbook, but he had to admit it was rather fun.

"I wonder if we can get those custom made," Witt ventured as Jana placed a tall stack of paper serving baskets into the cart. "You know, in blue with our name on them?"

The disapproving nose-wrinkle that had accompanied her earlier crack about the truck's paint job returned. "I wouldn't."

Well, points for honesty. "Too much?"

She sat back on one hip, eyeing boxes of plastic forks, knives and spoons. "It's not bad idea in and of itself—the visual of someone enjoying their burger with your logo close by is a good tactic. But you need to be careful with the color. Studies have shown that blue serving ware can actually be an appetite suppressant."

She really did know her stuff. "Now there's something they don't teach you in business school."

"The stuff next to the food?" she continued. "That ought to be white—or even yellow. Yellow makes food exciting and memorable." With that, she picked up a case of lemon yellow napkins. "Have you got a business card?"

"What?"

"A Blue Thorn business card. They're screaming blue, right?"

Screaming? Witt fished one—yes, definitely blue—business card out of his wallet and handed it to her. It occurred to him that he had not yet had any made for Jana. "Do chefs need business cards?"

"Not this chef. The coat's a perfect touch, but I don't need too many of the other bells and whistles. I don't want them, actually. My food does my networking for me." She eyed him. "Only I expect you've got an extensive marketing plan all laid out, don't you?"

He did—three versions. Witt had run his family's wholesale meat business—Star Beef—for years before his sister Mary's new husband had come in and taken over. That branch of the family business may not need him anymore, but he was ready to show what he could do with *this* branch.

He'd done his research, and he knew the basics of how food trucks operated. A loyal customer base following the truck's location was key to success. A surprisingly pretty chef wouldn't hurt that effort, either. "As a matter of fact, I do."

Jana held the business card up next to the yellow napkins. Even Witt could see that the blue and yellow went together well. The black and turquoise of the card popped against the yellow, while the yellow balanced out the bright hue of the blue card. "What do you think?" she said, squinting one eye in artistic consideration.

"I like it."

She raised a dark eyebrow. "Do we need to get approval from the rest of the company brass?"

"Huh?"

"Can I choose yellow napkins on my own or is that a corporate culture decision?"

This felt like another test as to how much artistic freedom she would have with the truck. He'd best step with care.

He made his voice dramatically formal. "Speaking as one-third of the executive branch, I'd say we can grant you authority on paper products."

Jana grunted as if she didn't find the joke as amusing as he did. After a sideways glance, she gave the color combination one final assessment and then put three more cases of yellow napkins in the cart. She put her hands on her hips. "That's it for basic supplies. Now let's get some ingredients."

Watching Jana browse through the grocery section of the store was just plain fun. She inspected every tomato and discarded two types of buns before choosing a third. "These are just for now, naturally. We'll want to choose a bakery vendor and get most of our produce from the market, that sort of thing."

"Of course," he said, only half understanding what she meant. He hadn't really thought about where cooks got their ingredients. While he had plenty of experience selling beef, it had always been in bulk quantities to major vendors, not smaller sales to individuals. But like other things, that was changing now that he was at Blue Thorn. Witt was already well underway firing up the Blue Thorn Ranch Store back in Martins Gap. While established in the wholesale business, Witt planned to have the Blue Thorn brand growing fast in local retail, and online, as well as expanding the wholesale market. His idea for a food truck presence selling bison burgers in downtown Austin was going to take everything to the next level. Sure, he was moving fast, but fast was his natural speed. Based on Jana's passion for basic but exceptional food, she was definitely the right chef for the job.

Back on the truck, the tiny space seemed to come alive once the supplies and ingredients were stowed on board. "Up until now, it just looked like a vehicle," he said as he tucked the aforementioned yellow napkins into the cabinet Jana selected. "All of a sudden, it looks like a restaurant."

Jana pulled an apron out of her messenger bag and spread her knife kit on the counter. With gleaming eyes, she said, "Now let's see if she *acts* like a restaurant. Regular burger or cheeseburger?"

Music to any hungry man's ears. "I like them both. You pick."

She leaned over to the below-counter fridge,

pulling out the packets of ground bison meat and running her hands over the three different kinds of cheeses she'd purchased before settling on the sharp cheddar. "Cheese. With grilled onions. And a special fix or two of my very own. Delicious," she added with something close to a wink, "but not adventurous."

"No Ugandan spotted goat curd?"

"Not on your life." She pulled out an onion and the monstrous brick of butter they'd purchased. With deft fingers, she turned the dial on the grill, changing the setting twice over the next two minutes. Then whatever she was waiting for seemed to arrive, and she tossed a spoonful of water on the grill.

The smile on her face at the sizzling sound matched the glow in his chest. It had begun.

Jana took a pair of burgers out of the packet, seasoned them with what could only be called a dramatic flourish, and set them on the grill. The scent that filled the truck was nothing short of sublime.

"Get ready, boss. I'm about to grill your socks off."

Watching her work, watching her move and test and turn and putter around the tiny kitchen, Witt believed her.

Chapter Two

"I've got to admit, it was incredible," Witt told Gunner and Ellie as he had dinner with them back out at the ranch forty miles northwest of Austin. "It was just like she said— a basic burger perfectly done. Charred just enough around the edges, the cheese at the perfect point of melting, mustard with just a bit of kick—everything." His mouth salivated just at the memory of the burger. If he could convince her to try just a few trendy items, go just a little beyond the basics, they'd be a hit for sure.

"I knew she'd be great," Ellie gloated. "Sure, she's an unknown now, but she won't stay that way."

"A pretty girl who can grill a great burger?" Gunner remarked. "Guys will line up around the block."

Ellie nudged him in reply. "Whoa there, brother. That's a rather sexist remark for a married man with a daughter and a new son. You make sure you teach Trey and Audie that it's what a woman *does*, not how she looks, that matters." She narrowed her eyes at him. "Or Aunt Ellie will come over there and do it for you."

"Yes, ma'am." Gunner nodded with a smile. "But come on, you can't argue that Jana adds to the appeal. Working a food truck, she needs to be as much saleswoman as chef. I know you're the one working the PR campaign, Witt, but folks have to like whoever's behind the counter."

"She can sell, I'm sure of it," Witt agreed. "She's easy to promote—I'm sure she looks great on camera, and that's an asset." Witt glanced over at Ellie. "Am I allowed to say that?"

"Yes, you're allowed to say that," Gunner answered before Ellie could. Sometimes the brother-sister tension with those two ran a bit strong. Gunner was clearly the boss—and always had been—but Ellie wasn't shy about asserting herself.

"You're right there. Jana's got loads of personality. She's the whole package," Ellie said as she sat back. "And yes, I will admit, most of the servers and even lots of the corporate staff back in Atlanta thought she was a looker." She pointed at Witt. "But that's not why we hired her. We hired her for her skills."

"Yes, we did," Witt agreed, the sensation of the perfectly melted cheese on his tongue still a vivid memory. Of course the food was the first priority. And he would have happily shared that tiny space with a burly guy who could cook as well as Jana. Still, any man with a pulse would concede that the scenery inside the Blue Thorn Burgers truck only added to the charm. "She has her share of opinions, too. And she isn't shy about sharing them. Kind of like the other woman in this company."

"Funny." Ellie gave Witt a look as she took another biscuit from the plate at the center of the table. "Did you have discussions, debates, or full-out arguments?"

"All three, I think, but it was okay. More like creative tension." He didn't mind being challenged if it led to better ideas and stronger business practices in the end. And he had a feeling most of Jana's ideas would be good ones. If they could strike a good working partnership, everything would work out fine. He was going to *make* this work, no matter what it took.

"Jana will take another couple of days to get the truck up and running, I'll hire one or two support workers..."

"Like Jose?" Ellie cut in. She'd insisted Witt hire one of the high school kids she and her fiancé, Nash, had met while running an after-school program for local at-risk teens. Ellie and Gunner cared a lot about what they did and how they did it. The Blue Thorn Ranch was about much more than the bottom line, which was what made it so satisfying to work with them.

"Like Jose," Witt replied. "I think he's coming down tomorrow. Are you sure the kid is okay staying with his brother down in the city? I mean, I'm all for giving kids opportunities, but a start-up food truck is going to call for long hours and hard work. Jose knows it won't be like some episode of a Food Network show, doesn't he?"

"Jose will be great," Gunner confirmed. "That kid's not one bit afraid of hard work. He's really grown up since graduation. I'd hire him on the ranch if we had work for him."

Despite Blue Thorn's long history, most of the recent changes—converting it into a bison ranch and expanding Blue Thorn Enterprises—made it feel more like a start-up.

Blue Thorn had run into some difficult times in the past few years under Gunner and Ellie's father, but the new generation of Bucktons were working hard to right the ship. It had its stresses, but Witt found it far more satisfying than the situation he'd left behind at home, watching his role at Star Beef get chiseled down to nothing by his sister and her ambitious new husband. Business was booming, as it had been for years, but he didn't feel wanted or accepted. And this was still family, after all—Witt's dad had been brother to Ellie and Gunner's father, Gunner Senior. This opportunity with his cousins at Blue Thorn had been an answer to his prayer, a place to show the world what he could do at a time when he was feeling truly stalled.

"If the food truck is successful, we could think of other mobile ventures," Ellie added. "I know of at least one yarn company that has a mobile store just like a food truck. We could do that here, you know."

"One expansion at a time, Els," Gunner said as he rolled his eyes. He turned to Witt. "The truck's own website and all that stuff is nearly ready?"

"It links right up with the ranch and store sites," Witt answered. Ellie did all the public relations for the consumer side, and the wholesale piece had been up and fully running without a hitch. "Two-thirds of your customers have converted to the online ordering system, and I'll be visiting the rest after we get the truck settled in. We're ready."

"And the social media? Twitter, Facebook, Insta-whatever, all that stuff?" Gunner asked.

"Instagram. Yes, we'll be hitting all that at full speed as soon as Jana gives the all clear," Ellie explained. "And Jose said he'd help, too. That kid would cut off his own arm before he'd put down his cell phone."

"We agreed—after a lively discussion, mind you—on a soft opening," Witt went on. "Showing up unannounced at a variety of places until we both are sure the product and the system are perfect."

"How close are you?" Gunner asked.

Witt took another biscuit himself. "That depends on who you ask. There was some *debate*—" he gave the word emphasis as he looked at Ellie "—as to the merits of long lines."

"Long lines?" Gunner questioned.

"I think long lines are great marketing. Makes you look like you're in demand."

Ellie raised an eyebrow. "And Jana?"

"She says a line can be long enough to put someone off. We settled on a goal of no more than six people waiting for the first two weeks, with an option to renegotiate."

Ellie frowned. "I know you. You've calculated a burger-per-hour profit ratio, haven't you?"

Witt stalled. "Well…maybe. We do need some benchmarks to shoot for. You can't tell me you didn't have goals like that back at GoodEats."

Ellie's expression told Witt just what she thought of such goals. "You've got nothing to worry about," she said. "That woman knows her stuff. You've already arranged to shoot some photos and videos the first week, haven't you? I predict Jana's going to be a hit."

"Like our burgers," Gunner chimed in.

"Exactly like our burgers," Witt agreed.

There was a pause in the conversation before Gunner shifted uncomfortably in his chair and said, "Your mom called." He said it softly, slowly, which told Witt he knew exactly what the admission implied.

"No kidding." Witt said. "Checking up on me now that I've jumped the family ship?"

"I told her you'd only jumped to a related shipping line. But yes." Gunner ran a hand across his chin. "She said your dad asked a lot of questions."

"What'd you tell her?"

"The truth," Gunner replied. "I told her Star Beef's loss was our gain. I told her I think Uncle Grayson will regret letting you leave."

"I still don't think he gets it," Ellie offered with compassion in her eyes. They'd talked long and hard about his moving to Blue Thorn. Ellie knew what it was like to grow up with fathers like the Buckton brothers and how chilly it could be in the shadow of the Eldest and Heir. His sister Mary had always been the eldest, but Witt had always dared to think he was at least partial heir to the ranch until Mary's high-powered husband, Cole Sullivan, entered the picture.

"Oh, I know. Dad thinks I ought to be thrilled to fall in line under Cole's breathtaking five-year plan." The bitterness in his own voice surprised him—Witt thought he'd made more peace with the issue than that. "It's not a bad plan," he admitted. "It's just that I'm not anywhere in it."

"Gran grabbed the phone out of my hand and gave your mom a piece of her mind," Gunner said with a smirk.

"I'd like to have been there for that." Witt could just picture Gran telling off her daughter-in-law. She'd have told off her son in stronger terms, come to think of it. Some days it was hard to imagine how two men as hard-headed as Gunner and Grayson Buckton had been the sons of the tender, caring woman all the cousins called Gran. Then again his grandmother Adele Buckton had a hard head and a stubborn will of her own to match her big heart—she just had the grace and compassion to be a lot more forgiving. "Gran will like Jana. They're made of the same stuff, I think."

"I agree," Ellie said, leaning in. "Why don't you invite her out to the house for a barbecue this weekend? She can meet the whole family. And see the bison." She suddenly reached for her handbag, rummaging through it until she produced her cell phone. "Never mind, I'll text her myself right now." After a minute of furious typing, Ellie smiled. "Done. Six o'clock, Saturday night. Jana's bringing coleslaw. You have not lived until you've tasted this woman's coleslaw."

Jana looked around the ranch Saturday night, taking in the scene spread out before her. She and Ellie were acquaintances—not good friends but friendly enough back when they'd worked together in Atlanta—but even though they hadn't been especially close, Jana had heard a few stories about the legendary Buckton family. Nothing had prepared her for this.

"You know," she said as she helped Ellie with a tablecloth, "I sort of get the whole color thing now." She'd seen the Buckton blue eyes before, of course, but seeing Gunner, Ellie, Grandmother Adele and Witt all together in one place, the family trait stood out like a neon sign. She'd tried not to fixate on the stunning nature of Witt's eyes, but with his hair—Gunner and Ellie had tawny-colored hair but Witt's was a darker shade, closer to brown—they were extraordinary. It made her disobedient brown curls and brown eyes feel mundane.

"I hated my eyes growing up," Ellie offered, shrugging. "Everywhere I went in town, everybody knew I was a Buckton, and I didn't always think that was such a good thing. Now," she said, her eyes straying to the man she'd introduced as her fiancé, "I find myself hoping that when Nash and I have kids, the blue shows up. At least in some of them."

"I'm glad it all worked out so well for you," Jana said. She remembered how worried she'd been about Ellie when she'd heard about the woman's spectacular breakup with star chef

Derek Harding. Not that Jana blamed her—if she'd caught her own fiancé kissing her best friend, she didn't know what she would have done. At least Ellie had had a place to go—back home to Blue Thorn. And it was Ellie's exodus from the trauma that she had to thank for the chance to meet Nash.

Jana was glad to make her own exodus away from Atlanta and the painful memories of Ronnie, even if it did mean leaving Mom behind. "I suppose I even owe my job to that happy outcome."

"I hope you get a happy outcome of your own. I think you'll do fabulously at the wheel of the Big Blue Bus."

Jana balked. "The Big Blue Bus?"

"Oh, that's just what my niece, Audie, called it the first time Witt brought it around. It sort of stuck. Don't tell Witt—he hates the nickname. It's the Blue Thorn Burgers truck—and maybe the first of many—as far as Witt's concerned. Has big dreams, our Witt does. He can be a bit too driven, if you ask me, but I think he'll settle down."

The last thing I need right now is another overdriven male, Lord. Keep me safe out here, Jana prayed as she began walking around the table setting out plates—turquoise plates. She caught Witt's eye when she first saw them. He shrugged as if to say, *I know what you said about eating off blue plates, but what are you gonna do?*

"Did you like the chef's coat?" Ellie asked, planting a big blue jug of yellow flowers in the center of the table. *See?* Jana wanted to say to Witt. *See how yellow balances all that blue out?*

"I've been meaning to thank you," Jana replied. "It's perfect. Really, just the right touch. The embroidery, the *female* fit, everything."

Ellie smiled. "You're welcome. I didn't want to leave that task to the boys. Who knows what you might have ended up wearing if I had?"

Dinner was a rowdy, pleasant family affair straight out of *Country Living* magazine. Gunner and his wife, Brooke, doted over their baby boy, the whole family making guesses as to whether one-month-old "Trey"—their nickname for Gunner Buckton III—would dare to have his mother's brown eyes instead of the family blue. Jana declined to vote when asked by Audie, Brooke's daughter, who adoringly called her stepfather "Gunnerdad."

"You're gonna drive the Big Blue Bus, aren't you?" the girl whispered as she slid onto the picnic table bench beside Jana.

"I heard that," Witt, seated across from

her, teased with mock seriousness. Well, *mostly* mock.

Audie rolled her big brown eyes. "The food truck."

"The Blue Thorn Burgers food truck," he corrected as he reached for the big bowl of coleslaw Jana had brought. "Ellie says your coleslaw is out of this world. Based on your burgers, I'm inclined to believe her."

"Do you like to cook?" Jana asked the little girl.

"I help Grannie Buckton with the cookies and brownies sometimes. I mostly like to draw, although Aunt Ellie taught me to knit and I like that, too."

Jana smiled. "Your aunt Ellie would teach everyone to knit if she got the chance. She taught lots of people back where we worked in Atlanta."

Audie scooped out a big helping of the coleslaw when Witt handed her the bowl. "Did she teach you, Miss Jana?"

"I haven't had time to learn yet. Besides, I'm not much for sitting down. I stand most of my day at work, and I like to run when I have free time." She threw a quick glance at Witt. "I'm thinking I won't have a lot of free time for a while."

"You can stand while you spin with a drop

spindle. Aunt Ellie taught me that, too. I can show you after dinner if you like. We use the bison fur to make the yarn you can buy at our store in town."

Jana laughed. "I see you have your cousin Witt's gift for public relations and persuasion."

Audie's cheeks turned pink. "That's what Gunnerdad says."

"Chef Jana's food *is* really good," Witt added. "Ellie was dead on about the coleslaw. What's in there to give it that…" he searched for a word "…zing?"

It never got old hearing people praise her food. She gave Witt a sly smile. "Wouldn't you like to know?"

"Secret family recipe?"

"Secret Jana recipe. I don't come from a cooking family." She didn't come from much family at all—divorced parents, an only child, no strong connections to aunts or uncles, no living grandparents. Yet when Jana discovered cooking through a high school class, the kitchen became the place where she felt most at home. *Any* kitchen where she could make her food. This whole big-family dynamic felt like a foreign country to her.

"You didn't eat in your family?" Audie asked, eyes wide.

Jana grinned at the girl. Looking around at the crowded table heaped with food, Audie must have found the concept impossible. "I didn't mean it that way. The people in my family cooked to feed themselves, but not much more." She picked up a piece of cornbread and held it up. "To me, cooking is art and science. It's a gift and an experience for people to share. I'm happiest when I make meals for people. Meals that make them smile and marvel and delight in the pleasure of great food."

"I like food," Audie replied. "And Cousin Witt's right—this is really good. If I were a cabbage, I'd be happy to be in this coleslaw."

Jana couldn't help but smile. "Well, that's about the best review I've ever had. Maybe we should post that on the side of the Big Blue Bus. 'Our coleslaw makes cabbages happy.'" She raised an eyebrow in challenge to Witt.

His eyes slanted. "How about we just tweet that one? By the way, we've got a photographer scheduled on Wednesday to take some shots of you and the truck. Promo stuff. You okay with that?"

Jana tried not to stiffen. Yes, it had been years since she'd had to deal with Ronnie and his harassment, but the fear remained, and the instinct to hide, to avoid putting her face or her name out there in a public way that might draw his attention again. "I'm not one for photos. Take all you want of the food or the truck, but skip the ones of me if it's all the same to you."

"Nonsense. We need at least a few shots of you. The pretty woman behind the burger grill? You're one of our best marketing hooks. We'll need three or four shots we can use. It won't hurt, I promise."

Jana tried to stifle her reluctance to being anyone's "hook" with the compliment he'd just paid her. It didn't work. "One."

"Two?"

"You're the prettiest chef I've ever seen," Audie offered, oblivious to the tension. "I think everyone should see your picture."

Jana tried to sigh rather than scowl. "Thank you, Audie, but I'm not big on publicity. I'd rather let my food get all the attention."

"So Wednesday's okay?"

It annoyed her how much he pressed the point, but she wasn't going to win this one. Not when surrounded by Bucktons. "Yes, Wednesday will be fine."

Chapter Three

Tuesday afternoon, Witt looked around at the full trash can and the truck's empty cupboards. "I think that went pretty well." They'd set up unannounced outside a group of office buildings at lunch hour, launching a two-hour "test run" to see how things worked.

"It could have gone better." Jana sat with her legs dangling out of the truck's open back door, her chef's coat unbuttoned to reveal a bright orange T-shirt, and a big mug of coffee in her hand. She wore a bright yellow scarf like a headband in a failing attempt to control the wild curls that kept escaping her piled-up hairstyle. Jana's hair held a troublesome fascination for him—the curls seemed to have a mind of their own, framing her face in a different way every time he looked at her. Right now they were plastered to her neck in a maze of circles that should have looked messy and sweaty but instead looked more mesmerizing than he would like to admit.

"Did you see how those guys ate your food?" Jose asked as he finished loading trash into a plastic bag. "You were a hit, Chef Jana." While Witt had harbored some doubts about Jose as kitchen help—the kid wasn't even six months out of high school—the boy had proven a hearty worker. He also spoke Spanish, which ended up being very useful with some of the office workers and many of the landscape workers from the park across the street. "I heard '*delicioso*' more times than I can count."

"The lines were too long. We need to streamline the prep process a bit." Jana squinted one eye in thought, as if already pondering tactics in her mind.

"No, no—the lines were great," Witt countered as he popped open a soda can and offered a second to Jose. "Lines let people know Blue Thorn Burgers are worth waiting for. Didn't we agree six people in line was okay?"

"For the first two weeks," she reminded him. "And we had more than six a lot of the time."

"That's not so bad, is it? This is our first real operational test."

Jana wasn't convinced. "Any more than six, and a customer's got too much time to change their mind." She swirled the last of her coffee and then drained the cup. "I think we can speed things up, though I have to admit, you were pretty fast at the cash register there, cowboy."

Working the register was the easiest way to track their sales per hour, but he wasn't going to tell her that. "That's me, master button-pusher." He sat down next to Jana. "I worked the counter at the local hardware store through high school. I work the counter at the Blue Thorn Store every now and again, too, just to get a feel for the customers. I was watching the customers today."

"I'd expect no less of you." It wasn't quite a jab, but close. "And what did you get a feel for?" She sat back against the door frame, defensive but clearly curious.

"I think we need a few more things to appeal to female customers."

That brought a look from her. "Watching the ladies, were you?"

"Watching the ladies *eat*, actually. The burgers seem too big for them. I was thinking maybe we need sliders."

Her head tilted dubiously to one side. "Sliders are trendy." It wasn't a compliment.

"Sliders are smaller, easier to handle. Same basic food, just a slightly different delivery. A plate of three sliders and slaw would sell well. We could play up the low-fat health benefits of bison meat, too. Do a two-slider or one-slider version as a kid's meal, even."

"Whatever you do, don't mess with the fries," Jose remarked as he leaned against the open door. "Those are awesome. What is that you put on them?"

"Wouldn't you like to know?" Jana teased. Hadn't she said the same thing to Ellie's inquiry of her coleslaw recipe? "Seasonings are my thing. It's what makes good, simple food great."

Jose preened the collar of his shirt. "I like a lady who knows how to be spicy."

Jana tossed a dishrag at the boy. "Every once in a while I forget you are a teenager—and then you remind me. I'll have none of that in my kitchen."

"Okay, okay." Jose held up his hands.

"Yes, Chef," Witt corrected.

"Yes, Chef," Jose relented.

Witt turned to Jana. "You're all set for tomorrow's photo shoot?"

Her eyes lost any sparkle. "I suppose."

"You act like I'm making you go to the dentist." With Jana's natural beauty, Witt couldn't imagine what would make her shy away from cameras.

"It's not my thing, that's all. Like I said, I prefer to let my food do the talking."

"I get that, but people connect to *people* as much as they do to food. The way you look, the way you talk about food, the connection you make with customers? All that is just as compelling as a great burger. You're highly promotable, Jana. That's a good thing. It's a strength we can use."

"That's marketing talk for 'you're pretty and guys'll like you,'" Jose said.

Jana gave Witt a dark look. "Is it?"

Witt knew this was thin ice, but he did want to get his point across. "Not in the way Jose thinks."

"So how does Witt think?"

Witt searched for the right words to compliment her beauty without insulting her talent. "You're unique. You don't look anything like the other guys hawking burgers around here. You are a beautiful woman and I'd like to think we can use that without getting stupid or exploitive about it. The fact is you look as good as you cook. Why can't that be a strength we can build on?"

"My man's got a point," Jose said as he leaned up against the truck door.

My man? Witt threw Jose a "don't get cocky" glare.

"Look, I don't want you to do anything that makes you uncomfortable. I don't want to cross any lines here. But the truth is that I can promote you just as easily as I can promote the food—maybe even easier. You make us unique in a way that people can see even before they taste your cooking."

He could see she was skeptical. "I promise, you'll have approval on every promotional shot that goes out," he went on. "This photographer, Mica? I've used her before. She can get shots that really let your personality shine through. We want to promote you for who you are—not just for the way you look. No one wants to turn you into a spokesmodel."

"But you could," Jose offered. "I mean, the whole hot-chef thing could…"

Witt cut Jose short by yanking the door, nearly sending Jose tumbling. "That's quite enough of that. You're done here. Why don't you head on back to your brother's and we'll see you tomorrow."

"Hey, sure. I'm gone." With that, Jose pulled off his apron, hopped on his bike and headed off down the street.

"Maybe I should have listened to my gut

and not hired him," Witt said as he watched the boy pedal off.

"He's fine," Jana dismissed. "He'll be good, actually. Hard worker, quick on his feet, and just the right amount of misplaced machismo to appeal to customers. We just need to tamp down the teenage-hormone factor."

Witt laughed, then turned to give Jana a serious look. "So we're okay on the photo thing?"

She rubbed a spot of sauce off her arm. "I'll get used to it."

"Mica will get it right, I promise you. It'll be as much about the food as about you." He paused before he added, "But really, you've got nothing to be nervous about for the pictures. You're…" He stopped short of paying her another compliment. He definitely found her attractive, but if that wasn't a recipe for bad choices in this setup, he didn't know what was. He settled on "You're just what we're looking for." Standing up, he retrieved his notebook and files from the truck's back counter. "You got the email from Mica to bring the chef's coat and two changes of street clothes? She wants some personal shots as well as some cooking ones."

"I got it." He sensed she still wasn't totally comfortable, but chose not to press it. Lots of women he knew got weird about having their picture taken, but none of them with less reason than Jana Powers. She was lovely, and Mica was friendly and encouraging. Tomorrow would be fun—Jana just hadn't realized it yet. He got the feeling that once she got over her needless self-consciousness, she would glow for the camera the same way she glowed behind the grill—vibrant and engaging.

He changed the subject. "Did you get the parking rental agreement from your building?" To his complete and delighted surprise, Jana had negotiated a great deal on parking the truck in her apartment building's lot in exchange for opening up on-site the first Saturday of each month. Marketing combined with operational savings—music to a number-cruncher's ears. Plus, it was much better than having to haul the truck back and forth from an industrial lot by his own apartment farther out of town where Witt had been parking it before.

"Right here." Jana pulled an envelope from her bag.

"This is an amazing deal," he remarked as he scanned the papers. "I would never have thought of this."

She smiled, some of the earlier tension leaving her face. "Makes for a blissfully short commute. And I can fuss around in the kitchen at midnight if I get a new idea."

"Night owl?" Most people in the restaurant business were, according to Ellie, who worked with lots of chefs and other food professionals.

"More like insomniac. I have one of those brains that rarely shuts down when it's supposed to."

There seemed to be a bit of a story behind that remark, but Witt chose not to pursue it. "I know how that goes. I've kept a notebook by my bed for years, and another one next to my rowing machine. I seem to get all my best ideas away from my desk."

"You crew?" she asked. "Or row just for exercise?"

"I was on the crew team all four years in college. Despite my height, I was never any good at basketball. Crew was the next-best place for a guy of my size."

"I had a friend who rowed in high school, and she got me involved, too." She met his surprise with a smirk—at her height she clearly wasn't tall enough to row. Maybe coxswain, though—those people who sat at the back of the boat and called out the strokes and directions were often small. "I got into it as a coxswain, not a rower," she added, confirming his guess. "That's where I honed my talent for barking orders."

His brain tried to conjure up an image of Jana perched on the edge of a rowing shell, gliding through the water on a misty morning, but he shut that attempt down as quickly as possible. Instead, he offered "Something else we have in common," then wanted to swallow back the remark. *Time to leave before you say something else stupid.* "Well, I'll see you tomorrow, then."

"Tomorrow."

Get your head in the right place, Buckton, Witt scolded himself as he walked to his SUV. He needed to make this food truck a success, to show his family—both at Blue Thorn and at Star Beef—that he could do this. An attraction to Jana put that goal at risk. He'd had employees before. He knew how to manage a staff without getting too attached. He had a feeling, however, that managing someone as strong-willed, attractive and off-limits as Jana Powers was going to be a whole new challenge.

Jana pulled in a deep breath Wednesday morning as she turned the truck into the parking lot of the address Mica had given her. It wasn't the turn that made her stomach tighten—she'd been surprised at how easily she'd picked up maneuvering the large truck—it was the task ahead of her.

Mica's studio was in a more industrial part of town, a renovated loft space that made for the perfect interior and exterior shots Jana knew Witt wanted. Witt was right; Mica sounded warm and artistic even in her emails. Someone she might even come to call a friend in this new city. So it wasn't the photographer that made her uneasy. In fact, it wasn't even the photographs. It was the prospect of publicity. Of being known by strangers. Coming back up out of the shadows where she'd hidden herself for years—that felt hard. Maybe she should have told Witt—or at least Ellie—about all the Ronnie business when they'd first talked about this job.

Why? It's not part of your work life. It's personal. And anyway, it's all in the past. You can do this. You need *to do this*, she told herself as she grabbed the extra clothing and opened the truck's back door. *Promoting is a huge part of Witt's overall plan, and you don't want start off messing things up with the new boss*. She'd paid her dues for years making boring food or pandering to owners who jumped on the latest food fad—this truck could be her chance to truly establish herself and her own personal style. It was worth a trip outside her comfort zone. *You've let Ronnie keep you in hiding long enough*, she chided herself as she stepped out of the truck. *I know You laid this opportunity at my feet, Lord*, she prayed. *Help me trust You with all of it. I don't believe You want me to live in fear any more than I want to keep looking over my shoulder.*

"Hey there!"

Jana jumped a foot before realizing it was Jose that had come around the corner of the truck. She'd been so startled she'd almost dropped her clothes onto the dirty asphalt.

Jose caught her bag just as it slipped from her shoulder. "Whoa, there. Didn't mean to freak you out. Witt told me to meet you here at 10:30 to wash the truck."

"I know. Sorry."

"Hey." Jose grinned. "It's only 10:28. I'm shocked that I'm early, too."

Jana tried to paste a casual smile on her face. "Good for you." She tossed him the truck keys. "There's a bucket and some sponges under the sink, and a ladder behind the door. Get her all ready for her close-up and come up to Mica's loft on the third floor when you're done, okay?"

Jose caught the keys in one hand. "Sure

thing, Chef." Witt had insisted Jose use classic kitchen protocol and reply "Yes, Chef" when responding to all her requests. It came out lots of different ways—things like "*Sí*, Chef," "Gotcha, Chef," and "Yep, Chef," which continually amused her. Sure, she'd been a bit put off by his wild-guy look with crazy long hair, and a large tattoo down one arm, but the truth was the kid had a sweet nature and a soft heart. He loved being here. He worked hard, too. She'd been startled at Ellie's recommendation of kitchen help at first, but could truly grow to like the guy.

"Go stun 'em in there," he called, waggling his eyebrows and even adding a wolf whistle as she turned toward the loft.

Jose's teasing struck an already raw nerve. She had to get over the way she dreaded this photo shoot. Restaurants were a PR-driven business—through advertising, social media, word of mouth, or hopefully all three. It was clear Witt expected her to give interviews, and pose for photos with her burgers and the bright blue truck. Witt had every right to expect her to be ready and eager to do all those things. And really, what was there to be so upset about? She was about to get her hair and makeup done by a professional stylist and enjoy the glamor of a photo shoot—most woman would relish this experience.

You're not shy, she told herself as she pulled open the large metal doors to Mica's building. *You were scared once, but that's not the same thing. And you don't have to be scared anymore. Ronnie Taylor is hundreds of miles from here and years in your past. Don't you dare let that that creep steal your present or your future. You walk in that room as Chef Jana, Austin's next food sensation.*

As the metal box of an elevator groaned its way to the third floor, Jana straightened her shoulders, lifted her chin and inhaled all the way to her toes. *I will live in fierce expectation of all God has planned for me,* she recited, a favorite quote her mom had sent her in card after card during cooking school and beyond. Right along with the verse from Jeremiah 29:11— *"For I know the plans I have for you," declares the Lord, "plans to prosper you and not to harm you, plans to give you hope and a future."*

Jana's hope and future were waiting up there on the third floor, and in the bright blue truck that stuck out like an aqua sunbeam in the parking lot below. She yanked open the elevator's cage door with a deliberate gusto and let herself feel excited at the scene before her.

Mica's loft looked exactly as Jana had imagined—a huge industrial space strewn with equipment, drapes, fans and props as well as an artfully decorated living space tucked in one corner. Swingy, energetic Americana jazz filled the sunlit space. Mica looked up from a tripod to wave eagerly at Jana.

"And there she is," Witt called out from a counter where coffee and some bagels were set out. "Our star."

"Her and the dozen burgers she's going to make me," Mica offered. "Oh, I do love the jobs where I can eat the props when we're done." She walked up to Jana. "Hang those clothes on the rack and grab yourself some coffee. Linda's just getting set up over there." The stylist looked up from her bag and waved just as Mica had done. "That woman's a wonder," Mica said as she leaned in. "I'd give anything to have her in my bathroom every morning doing my hair and makeup." She winked. "I'd probably be on my fourteenth wedding proposal by now if I did. Not that you need much primping, sugar. Witt wasn't lying when he said you were the whole package. That hair…" She ran her eyes over Jana's mass of unruly curls as if they were strewn with diamonds. "Linda, honey, will you come look at this hair?"

"I can see it from here," Linda replied. "Finally, the Good Lord sends me something I can work with!"

The pair of them plied Jana with compliments and encouragement for the next half hour, until Jana rose from the chair feeling like a beauty queen. She was going to have to get Linda to show her how she could do her eyes like this at home, because they looked twice their size and doubly bright. As she slipped on the chef's coat, Jana felt beautiful. She tried to ignore the way Witt looked at her as she settled onto an ornate wrought iron stool sitting in front of a bright blue drape, but it was almost impossible.

"Va-va-va-voom!" Linda called as she stood behind Mica. "If you can cook as good as you look right now, honey, Blue Thorn Burgers is bound for success."

"She can," Witt replied. "And we are." The resolute tone in his voice sent a little flip through Jana's stomach that had nothing to do with anxiety.

"Turn the music up a notch," Mica said, pointing Witt over to the stereo in the corner. "Let's have some fun."

She *did* have fun. Jana surprised even

herself by enjoying the whole morning. She laughed, posed, climbed up on the truck, even got a bit goofy by the end as she mugged behind the line of twelve burgers she'd cooked up during the shoot. Jose was singing along with the radio by the end of the shoot, flirting with Linda, who was old enough to be his mother. When they all five of them sat down at the big table in the loft to "eat the props" as Mica had said, it had the feel of a family picnic rather than a dreaded promotional task.

"You were amazing," Witt exclaimed just before his eyes fell closed in carnivorous bliss as he bit into a burger. "This is amazing," he said after chewing. "I keep thinking I'll get used to it, but your burgers are still incredible every time I eat one."

"A gorgeous woman who makes burgers like these? It won't be me getting fourteen marriage proposals—you'll be getting a dozen a day."

Jana felt her cheeks color. "I doubt that. I'll settle for regular customers, thanks."

"Oh, you'll get 'em," Mica said, licking stone-ground mustard from the corner of her mouth. "Trust me, they'll be lining up for these." She peered at the burger. "I'm eating buffalo? Really?"

"Bison," Witt replied. "It's better for you than beef, you know."

Jose rolled his eyes. "Don't let him get started. He can go on for hours."

Everyone laughed. Jana looked around the room and allowed herself the pleasure of seeing her new friends enjoy her cooking. *A hope and a future indeed. Look out, Austin. Here we come.*

Chapter Four

Thursday afternoon, Witt took Jana back out to Martins Gap to see the ranch again. It was fun to watch her take in the spectacular scene that was the Blue Thorn Ranch bison herd out in their pasture. He'd borrowed Gunner's field truck to take her out into the fields—one simply didn't stroll out into the open fields to pal around with thousand-pound animals—so she could really see what made the ranch unique. It's the one thing they hadn't had time to do when she'd come for the earlier dinner, and being out in the open fields was a whole different experience than sitting around the family ranch house.

"Wow," she exclaimed, fighting to keep the breeze from sending her hair over her face as they sat in the back of the pickup and watched the herd. "They really are amazing."

He knew Jana was a city girl, but he could tell she caught the splendor of ranch life. It was all over her face as they watched the large brown-furred creatures meander among the tall grasses.

Witt tipped his hat back as he took in the wide horizon. "I could recite paragraphs to you about how the family groups are preserved, or how the harvesting is done in deliberately stress-free ways, and a bunch of other organic industry buzzwords, but I figured this was better. Whenever the business gets to me, I come out here for a few hours and get my head back on straight. Used to do it on my family ranch, too."

Jana fished a hair elastic out of her jeans pocket and pulled her curls back into a haphazard ponytail. A tiny bit of Witt regretted the confinement—Jana's hair in the wind was an enthralling thing, tumbling around her face and neck in a most distracting way. On second thought, maybe it was for the best that she'd tied it back. He should be glad her hair always had to be up and controlled in the food truck. When she'd worn it down for some of the more personal shots back in the photo studio, he'd had to force himself to stop staring.

"This isn't your family ranch?" she asked once the curls were under submission.

He'd wondered when he'd have to explain the course of events that had brought him to Blue Thorn. This seemed as good a place as any to tell the tale. "You know Gunner and Ellie are my cousins. My dad, Grayson Buckton, was Gunner Senior's younger brother. At one time they both lived on this ranch, back in the days when this was a big cattle operation."

"Gunner said something about revitalizing the ranch when he brought the bison on. So it used to be a cattle ranch?"

"Yes. And back then, it was twice, maybe three times the size it is now."

Jana let out a low whistle. "That must have been a sight to see. Like something out of a Hollywood Western."

"*Exactly* like that. The Bucktons go back four generations in these parts. Gran could tell you stories from back in the day that sound as if they came straight out of an old movie."

Gran had taken to Jana right away during that first dinner on the ranch. The 85-year-old matriarch of the family, who still lived on the land with Gunner Jr., welcomed Jana into the Blue Thorn fold with her trademark hospitality. "She seems like quite a woman, your grandmother," Jana remarked.

"Oh, she is," Witt agreed. "Strongest woman I know. It tore her up when her boys fought and my dad took his part of the herd and split off to make his own way." He waved off an insect that buzzed beside him. "Bucktons can be a headstrong, stubborn lot."

Jana gave him a sideways smile. "Can they? I hadn't noticed," she teased. The day of the photo shoot had gone wonderfully, but yesterday not so much. The weather had been hot and humid, and the truck's close quarters had fermented a spat between them over menu pricing. It was threatening to break out into an open argument when he'd called a truce and announced that they needed a "field trip" out here. The whole disagreement seemed petty now that they were out in the breezy pasture, where the glory of God's nature put everything in perspective.

"So your dad raises cattle, too?"

There was the sticking point. "And he's really good at it—to be honest, he was always better at it than his brother. Dad went off to grow Star Beef into one of the largest ranches in the next county while his elder brother, Gunner, stayed on the Blue Thorn and slowly ran it into the ground." He shot Jana a look. "You can imagine the family arguments that spawned. The tension between the brothers just grew worse and worse. By the time Gunner Senior died, I don't think he and my dad had said three words to each other in five years. They never reconciled, and I think it breaks Gran's heart to this day."

There was a bit of a pause before Witt continued, "Go ahead, ask it."

"Ask what?" she said, unsuccessfully hiding the question he could see in her eyes.

"Why am I here and not there?"

She looked down at her boots. "I wasn't sure it was any of my business."

Witt shifted against the side of the truck and looked out at the herd. "I had always planned to stay. My older sister, Mary, and I ran a lot of the day-to-day operations as Dad stepped back." He reached for the right words to relay the next part—it still wasn't easy to tell. "Then Mary married a guy from another huge ranch nearby, and, well, he sort of stepped right into the helm of Star Beef like he owned the place."

"Ouch," Jana said softly. "Didn't your dad have anything to say about that?"

Ouch indeed. Jana had hit on the most painful part of the story. "He had the opposite reaction, actually. Cole is very driven and comes from a powerful family. Cole's older brother runs his family's ranch, and I think

Cole was as bent on outdoing his brother as Dad was determined to outshine Gunner. Dad and Cole took to each other right away, as you can imagine. My role in the company got downgraded over and over again, and pretty soon it wasn't hard to see the writing on the wall. I wasn't that keen on spending my life playing second fiddle to Cole. When Gunner and Ellie came to me and asked about working at Blue Thorn, I saw it as a chance to make my own mark."

"How does your dad feel about that?"

Witt shifted his weight. "Let's just say it's not everyone's favorite topic of conversation. I don't think we'll see him lining up at the food truck, that's for sure. My guess is that he's waiting for it to fail and for me to come back with my tail between my legs. I reckon he thinks the whole thing is a silly fad for gullible city folk, and that it'll never amount to a real business."

"That's not true," she shot back. Witt liked the defiance in her voice. She really was the best person for the job. God sure had sent him exactly what he needed—even if it was nothing like he'd expected—with Jana Powers, hadn't He?

"No, it's not," he agreed. "I think the one truck is just the beginning. I think Blue Thorn could be the best thing to ever happen to Martins Gap. It was, once, and I hope we make it that way again."

Jana sat back. "That's a lot to heap on a butcher shop, a yarn shop and a burger truck."

"Well," Witt replied as he looked out over the pasture, "nobody said we were gonna do it the easy way."

Friday morning, Jana held up the truck's smart phone, the message typed in and ready to go. "Are you ready?"

Witt actually looked as anxious as she was. "As ready as I'll ever be. I've got sixteen people lined up ready to pass it along the minute it goes out."

Jana bit her lip. "I've got seventeen."

Jose piped in from the computer tablet mounted the truck's back wall. "And we've got a total of twenty people following our page so far."

"That's..." Jana fought the urge to count on her fingers—math had never been her specialty.

"Fifty-three people ready to spread the word," Witt finished for her. "Not much, but it's a start. Do it."

Jana held her breath, shot up a wordless plea to the Lord, and pressed Post. She imagined the message Blue Thorn #Burgers 7th & Brazos 11:30 winging its way through cyberspace to the small band of people they'd recruited to resend the truck's daily location out across several social media outlets.

After the photo shoot, Witt had arranged for Blue Thorn Burgers's social media addresses to be painted beside the truck's side counter window. Jana had come up with the idea to have the information printed right on the yellow napkins. If everything worked the way it was supposed to, the internet "word of mouth" would build their customer base—*if* they could deliver on a great eating experience to those who showed up today. They'd arrive at the stated destination in enough time to throw the counter windows open at 11:30 and serve whoever was waiting.

If anyone was waiting at all.

The whole thing made Jana's stomach churn with a mixture of energizing excitement and paralyzing fear.

Witt caught her expression. "It'll work," he said, as if he could hear the unspoken doubts clanging around her brain. "You're ready."

"I know *I'm* ready," Jose said, flexing his biceps. "*Vamanos.* Bring it on."

Witt slid behind the wheel. "Bring it on indeed." With that, he twisted the keys in the ignition and the truck roared to life.

The ten-minute drive to the intersection they'd chosen felt like it took ten hours. Jana mentally ran through preparations and menu items, praying for…she didn't really know what. People to be there? People to like the food? No mishaps? Not to run out of food? All of the above? It was as if her brain could concoct so many scenarios requiring God's immediate intervention, she didn't know which to form into prayers. She finally settled on "Just be there," breathing it in and out, letting it shape her focus as the truck turned the final corners.

Witt let out a low whistle. Was that good or bad?

Before the truck came to a stop, she launched up out of her seat to peer at the intersection through the truck's wide front windshield. The joyous sight of two dozen people pointing and waving sent a surge of relief through her body. Hungry, excited people. Waiting for her food. There wasn't a better sight in all the world.

"It worked." Witt exhaled. For all his confidence, his tone held the same relief she felt. "Customers." He looked back over his shoulder as he pulled the truck into position, his eyes glowing as bright as the truck's paint job. "So, Chef, you ready to feed some people?"

She had already turned on the grill. "Am I ever. You ready, Jose?"

Jose grinned as he started unloading condiments from the cabinet. "Yes, Chef!"

The next two hours flew by in seconds. Witt worked the cash register, feeding her tickets with orders. Her brain slid easily into the place where cooking became everything—where the sizzle of the meat met the warming bread under her hands and she orchestrated the movement of ingredients into place. There was nothing like this, no other place or activity that seeped so deeply into her soul and made her feel larger than life, vibrant, physically tingling from excitement and purpose.

The truck broiled from the grill heat and the strong fall sunshine. The little fans set up around the truck tried in vain to keep the air moving. She should have been miserable, hot and sweaty as she was, but Jana never noticed the heat. Only when she slid the last meal—a set of three "sliders" she'd relented and added to the menu at Witt's insistence—across the counter, did she recognize her body's exhaustion. It wasn't the bad, emptied-out kind of weary, however. Instead, it was a satisfying, used-up kind of tired. The sensation of giving all she had to give in the one place she knew she was meant to be.

Jana leaned against the back counters, her headband soaked, her chef's coat spattered and sticking to her arms. "Wow." She laughed, downright giddy at the thought of so many happy mouths fed. "It worked."

Witt slid the cash register drawer closed, practically slumping over it himself. "It did." He was sweaty, too—and smiling and laughing, clearly as pleased with how their first "announced appearance" had gone. His eyes held a playful challenge as he asked, "We sold out of sliders, didn't we?"

"That was the last one," she admitted. He'd been right; she could craft a basic trio of the smaller burgers without feeling like she'd given in to some trendy fad.

Jana waited for him to crow, *I told you so*, but instead he merely offered her a warm smile and wiped his forehead with a sleeve. "I knew you could do it."

It proved the perfect thing to say. Suddenly the long negotiations over whether to offer the sliders melted away, and she saw a glimpse of what she had hoped to find all along: a partnership. There was a long moment where they simply looked at each other, both soaked and exuberant, each a bit stunned that the whole thing had gone as well as it had. This was the last step, the truck's final test before they went into the full swing of daily operations next week. Blue Thorn Burgers was here. They had done it. Jana wanted to dance in the tiny truck corridor, to fling herself into a group hug with Witt and Jose, and to fall into an exhausted heap against the coolness of the refrigerator, all at once. Instead, she just stood there, alternately glancing at Witt and closing her eyes, laughing softly as she tried to get her hair back up off her neck.

Jose, who'd been ping-ponging his glance back and forth between his two bosses, finally threw up his hands. "Is anyone gonna check the feed?"

He grabbed the truck's tablet from its bracket on the wall and swiped through the menu until he found the Blue Thorn Burgers social media page. "We're up to eighty-five followers on Twitter, a hundred and twenty-six on Instagram. People have posted three videos, and there are sixty-two mentions on Facebook. And twenty-one…wait, now twenty-two five-star reviews on Yelp!"

Witt gave a whoop worthy of a rodeo cowboy. Jose high-fived Jana with a string of Spanish exultations, and Jana felt her chest glow in gratitude. She'd worked at restaurants before, but here, now, was the first true public applause for specifically and exclusively *her* cooking. For her as a chef. She'd been so afraid to be "known," to be out in the public eye for so many years, that she'd forgotten how gratifying the spotlight could feel.

Thank You, she prayed silently, her hand falling to cover her thumping heart. *Thank You.*

She opened her eyes to see Witt staring at her. The gratitude, the jubilant satisfaction that sparkled within her, was there in his eyes, as well. After all, he had as much at stake today as she did. "Thank you," she said, thinking the pair of common words entirely insufficient.

"My pleasure," he said. He held her eyes for one long moment more before sending a smirk Jose's way. "Hang on tight. I'm thinking it only goes up from here."

Chapter Five

Boring. The word gaped out like a sinkhole in the center of Jana's phone screen Tuesday morning. Of all the criticisms she thought she could stomach, this was the one that cut deepest. Boring. Could internet food critic "Spatula Dave" have said anything worse? They hadn't even invited any critics or bloggers this weekend just to avoid this kind of thing. She sank down onto the truck floor with her back against the counter. The coffee beside her tasted sharp and sour where five minutes ago she'd found the blend particularly smooth.

She scrolled through the other comments from Dave's followers, several of whom had visited the truck during its weekend operations. There were compliments scattered among the responses from people who disagreed with his assessment. And Dave didn't hate everything—he thought the coleslaw was particularly well-done. She noted, with an extra-sharp sense of annoyance, that he found the slider trio "a near miss." Witt would surely note that the most positive comment about a burger was given to the sliders. Her own creations? They hadn't fared nearly as well. The "I'm all alone here" feeling that had been fading now roared right back up with this setback.

Jana told herself to put the phone down, to stop hurting her heart by scrolling and re-scrolling across the article as if she were grabbing a hot pan over and over. *It's one person's opinion*, she told herself. *Yeah, one person who has an audience of*—she made herself scroll down to where the blog's fifteen-thousand-member following was listed—*too many*.

They'd done a bustling business their first official weekend, and there had been plenty of positive comments from satisfied customers on various restaurant review sites. Until this morning, Jana had felt she was riding on a wave of success.

A knock came on the back of the truck and Witt shook off his umbrella as he came in the back of the truck. One glance at her face must have told him all he needed to know. "So you saw."

Jana set the phone down on the floor beside her. "Hard not to." Maybe scanning the internet for mentions of the truck every morning wasn't such a good idea.

"It isn't all...bad." He hesitated before the final word. "He gave the truck three out of five stars." His tone was a last-ditch kind of hopeful, as if he knew his words wouldn't make up for what she'd read. "He liked the coleslaw."

"He liked the sliders...sort of." Jana tried to keep the edge out of her voice, but her comment still sounded like a pouty toddler's. Rejection—her Achilles' heel since Ronnie's torrent of put-downs and degradations— stung worse than anything.

Witt slid down to sit with his back against the opposite wall. "We'll get other great reviews, you'll see."

Jana hated to be so obvious in her need for reassurance. "I suppose."

"Hard to keep perspective at the moment, I get that."

She looked up into his eyes, still brilliant blue in the gray light coming through the truck windows. "Boring. I think I could take any criticism but boring. I would have been happier if he'd hated them. At least then I'd know I'd evoked a passionate response."

Witt laughed softly. "Jana Powers, believe me when I tell you, you are anything but boring. You're the opposite of boring. There isn't a single thing about you or your cooking that's boring."

She gave him a "nice try" look and swallowed more coffee.

"He's an idiot. Probably eats chicken nuggets and cold cereal on his days off. He's probably one of those guys who feels like he's not a real food critic if he doesn't hate something. And that's just it—he's not a real food critic. He's one guy with a cell phone and—"

"And fifteen thousand people who read what he thinks," she finished for him. "That's fifteen thousand people who aren't going to risk their money on a boring burger."

"And..." Witt scrolled down through his own phone, lips moving slightly as he counted something. "Fifteen of the twenty-two people who left a comment saying they'd come to the truck themselves argued that they liked what they ate. Two more say they are at least going to try us out."

"That's not a rave," she muttered.

"No, that's a conversation. The more comments, the higher up on the internet food chain this blog goes. People are talking about us, Jana, and that's what matters. If I read all these comments about an interesting new place to eat, I'd want to come try it out for myself and see which side I'm on."

She gave him a dark look. Why was Witt trying to put a positive spin on this? There wasn't any way to make this easier to swallow. "You wouldn't be more inclined to come over if Spatula Dave had boasted we fed him the best burger he'd had in years?"

"Stop. What if Spatula Dave has emotional baggage here? What if his grandfather was killed in a buffalo stampede? Or someone else's bad burger landed him in the ER with food poisoning?"

He was being purposefully melodramatic, and while his theory started the smallest part of a smile deep down inside, the grin couldn't find its way to her face. "If he hated burgers, he wouldn't be Spatula Dave."

Witt got up. "Lots of foods are cooked with spatulas. Pancakes, for example."

"We are not adding pancakes to the menu."

He extended a hand. "I'm not talking about the truck here. I'm talking about breakfast. What did you eat for breakfast?"

She didn't see the relevance. "Yogurt."

"Ick. Never liked the stuff. I declare the

need for a corporate meeting over pancakes. It's raining, so there's no point in going out to the park today. Jose has a doctor's appointment, so we're going to breakfast. No is not an option."

She looked up at him. What enabled him to slough this off so easily? "If he'd made some crack about the truck being too blue, you wouldn't be in the mood for pancakes." Spatula Dave had trashed her cooking. She had no choice but to take it personally.

Witt narrowed one eye. "Clearly, you haven't read AustinDine." He scrolled through his phone. "'No points for subtlety. The truck is a shocking blue that may even glow in the dark.'"

Ouch. "No," she admitted as she tried not to laugh at his wince, "I hadn't seen that one." So she wasn't the only one to suffer a few online dings right where it hurt the most. "For what it's worth, I've changed my mind about the blue. I think the color works. It's loud, but it works."

Witt's eyebrow rose. "Didn't expect that from you."

"I've never met a family with a signature color before. It took a little getting used to." She motioned to his eyes. "Does everybody have them? The Buckton blue eyes, I mean."

He shrugged. "Pretty much. Obviously, people who marry into the family don't, but it seems to be a stubborn gene. Even Bucktons who marry brown-eyed folks still get the blue eyes in their children. I think the genetic line knows better than to try to go rogue on this family."

Suddenly, she was curious. "Is it weird? Ellie said she didn't like having something that let everyone know who she was before she told them. Have you heard 'Oh, you must be a Buckton' your whole life?"

"I never really thought about it that way, but I suppose so." He shifted against the counter, running a hand through his brownish hair. "It's not quite the same back home since Star Beef's operation doesn't have the same history as the Blue Thorn. But I look a lot like my dad, and most people know who the Bucktons are, both in my hometown and in Martins Gap, so I guess I've never known what it's like to be anonymous."

They were so different. Maybe that's why he took so easily to publicity—he'd been public, thanks to his family, every day of his life. Part of her move from Atlanta had been to start over with none of the baggage of her previous life. To be, in some ways, anonymous.

"Haven't you ever wanted to just go somewhere where no one knows who you are?"

Witt shook his head and laughed softly. "That's more Gunner's thing. At least, it used to be. He and his dad used to butt heads all the time, and as soon as he was old enough, he left Blue Thorn behind, and started over fresh. He chose to be a rebel, and he excelled at it—until he came back, that is, to take it all over when his father died. I have to say, I admire the guy for turning his life around the way he did." His eyes grew distant, with just enough of a flinch to let Jana know this was a tender subject. "No, I've always been proud to be a Buckton. I think that's part of my problem, actually. Hard to take pride in a long family history when someone comes in and hijacks it for themselves."

Jana could see how deep that wound ran. To be that loyal, and then to be supplanted by a brother-in-law like Cole? Grayson Buckton should be ashamed of himself for discarding his son's fidelity the way he had. She'd never met Mary and Cole, but she'd have a hard time making peace with the way they'd ousted Witt. That was probably unfair of her, but looking at the shadow that fell over Witt's eyes when he talked about Star Beef or anything touching on his departure, Jana couldn't help it.

"Let's go get some pancakes," she said. "I heal better on a full stomach."

Witt should have known taking Jana to a restaurant would be an interesting experience. She took in every detail, analyzed everything from the menu paper to the syrup containers. He had the feeling there would never be anything close to a "normal meal out" with her, ever.

"They need better syrup," she said as she tried a third flavor of syrup on her buckwheat pancakes. "The pancakes are really good, but they're messing them up with lackluster syrup."

Lackluster? To him it was just breakfast. "I've always liked their pancakes here." Earlier he'd had the notion to have her over to grill a pair of steaks one weekend, but he was suddenly wondering if his pride could take a blow if his efforts at the barbecue fell under the same scrutiny she was currently giving her breakfast.

"Oh, they are good." Jana continued analyzing. "The texture's just right, and all that. Which is why the syrup shoots them in the foot."

"*Can* you shoot a pancake in the foot?" he teased.

She gave him one of her looks. He was getting to know her different glares, gaining a sense of which meant *very funny* and which meant *back off.* He never wanted to say anything to actually offend her, but when he aimed a zinger just right, she was fun to tease—it brought out a lighter, softer side of her that almost never came out when she was cooking. When Jana was cooking, she was like a comet shooting through the kitchen; bright and fiery, leaving a long trail of sparkles wherever she went.

"Feel better about Spatula Dave?" he dared to ask.

Jana sat back. "Yeah. I suppose everyone can't love us right away."

"But everyone *will* love us eventually," he replied, dousing his pancakes with another wave of "lackluster" syrup.

"Everyone, huh?"

"World domination through bison burgers. That's my plan, and I'm sticking to it."

Witt was glad to see her laugh. "And what, exactly, does world domination look like for Blue Thorn Burgers? Because I know you have it all planned out. In excruciating detail, I expect."

Now, there was a question to get a man up in the morning. He'd talked in vague terms about future expansion, not wanting to overwhelm her when they were just getting started, but a part of him had been waiting for her to ask this. Witt took the first syrup pitcher and placed it squarely between them. "We start with one truck. Get it just right, generate some excitement and a loyal following.

"Then," he went on as he picked up the second syrup pitcher, "when the lines get too long…"

She raised an eyebrow at that particular sticking point, but said nothing.

"When they get too long, we add another truck. Only that's tricky, because we'd need another Jana to run it. We've got to start looking long before we need her because the chef is the key to everything."

Witt watched her eyes glow at the compliment. It wasn't false praise—he really did feel Jana's personality and expertise were absolutely essential to Blue Thorn Burgers's success. "Hire another female chef?" she asked carefully.

"It'd be my preference." He paused just a moment before adding, "I think we're on to something special here. I really just want the chef who will do exactly what you're doing. I'd be okay if it were a guy, but somehow I think it might have to be a woman behind the counter to keep going what we've got."

He watched her take in all he'd just said, then picked up a third pitcher. "When those lines get too long, we add a third truck."

"Three trucks?"

"I like to think big." Witt caught her eye one more time before picking up the napkin container and placing it at the end of the little line of syrup pitchers. "Then, we go hard walls. A true brick-and-mortar restaurant."

"Really?" She looked surprised.

"Yeah, really. You didn't expect that?" Wasn't that what every chef dreamed of—running their own restaurant? Jana was way too talented to dream small. He wasn't sure if it was safe to say something like that—she always got so weird about compliments.

"Well…" She put her hand on the napkin container, twisting it this way and that as if inspecting the restaurant it represented. "I've heard you talk about expansion, but mostly in more general terms. I never realized you had in mind an actual restaurant."

"Isn't that the natural progression?"

"Not for a ranch marketing campaign." Her eyes widened, as if she hadn't meant to put it quite so bluntly.

Witt sat back in the booth. "That's what

you think the Blue Thorn Burgers truck is? A marketing stunt? One giant edible gimmick to hype the ranch?" It sounded like such a sleazy ploy when put like that. As if he and Gunner and Ellie hadn't ever taken it seriously. "Why would we hire someone like you if we thought of our trucks as just—" he reached for the right description "—nothing more than rolling billboards?" How had she missed his vision for all this?

"I don't know," she said, her tone vague and apologetic as if she couldn't think of any other response. That wasn't like Jana—she had an opinion on just about everything, especially when it came to her work. She was the last kind of person he'd expect to sign on to something she believed to be just a long-term PR tactic. How could someone with such a strong sense of her own skills be so quick to sell herself short? The contrast—like so much of her—didn't match up in any way he could understand.

Witt looked her straight in the eye. "We hired you. Your skill, your talent, your personality, your style. And not just to cook in a truck. Not just to cook in two trucks or even three. Jana, I'm sorry if somehow I didn't make you understand the future we want you to have here. I thought that was one of the big reasons you came on board, even though we certainly can't match the manpower or equipment you'd be used to in a full restaurant kitchen. It's why I'm so big on promoting you."

She looked a bit startled, as if this was all news to her. And that roiled in his gut, because he hated the idea of Jana selling herself so short. He hated that she thought of *him* as the kind of guy who thought like that. It did explain her resistance to all his efforts to promote her, though, and he was glad to put that misconception to rest. "We believe in you and what you can do." It felt overdramatic to put it that way, but now was no time to mince words.

She looked down for a moment, fussing with the silverware before looking back up to say, "Thank you," in a quiet tone he'd never heard from her before.

He offered her a smile. "I want the kind of chef who is so committed that one bad comment on Spatula Dave can send her into a pout, but I hate the idea of you taking all the dings so personally like that. We're going to get negative reviews. They're part of the business. And you can let it bug you, but not too much, okay?"

He was glad to see a slip of a smile return to her face. "Okay. But next time I pick where we get our pancakes."

Chapter Six

"A picnic forty miles outside of town?" Jana planted her hands on her hips. She was ticked. Witt had thought she'd welcome the chance to do something friendly and community focused like catering the Martins Gap Community Church All Saints' Day picnic two Sundays from now.

"Don't you think we ought to be staying in Austin on weekends to build our customer base?"

"We *are* building a customer base," he retaliated, getting defensive. "We're out here every day—and a lot of the people who live and attend church in Martins Gap work here in Austin." He hadn't expected such resistance, and he'd already promised the truck's appearance.

"Our base isn't strong enough yet to fend off dings like Spatula Dave's."

She'd been stuck on that one idiot's "boring" comment for three days. This wasn't her first job in the food service industry. She should have grown the required thick skin by now.

Eventually, he managed to convince her that they couldn't back out from the commitment to the church, but that didn't mean she was happy about it. From there, the "discussion" dissolved into an argument over photographs of menu items—he wanted them and she didn't. They'd been arguing for ten minutes, and Witt wasn't finding any way out of the spat. Finally, Jana turned around to glare at him. "Name the most basic food you know. One you like. One that's made, not an apple or a banana or something you just grab and eat."

His first thought was pancakes, but they'd already covered that ground. He pondered for a moment, then replied, "Grilled cheese."

The answer seemed to fit what she was looking for—whatever that was. "Okay, good. Now close your eyes."

He shot her an "I'm in no mood to play games" look, but she only glared at him harder, her eyes huge and her gaze commanding. Since she had all the sharp, heavy implements at her disposal while he could only reach the napkins, Witt relented. He shut his eyes with all the dramatic reluctance of a four-year-old, and bit back the urge to stick out his tongue.

"Tell me about grilled cheese," she said. Her voice told Witt she'd moved closer. He heard the scrape of the truck's little metal stool being moved, and then felt her hands on his shoulders pushing him to sit down. He almost did stick his tongue out, feeling like a little boy being told to go sit in the corner. "Remember eating a really great grilled cheese sandwich and tell me about it."

"I can't wax poetic about bread and cheese," he protested, feeling weird about the whole exercise but ready to admit it was at least better than the argument.

"I didn't ask you to. Just talk." He heard the rapid-fire snaps of the pilot light starting up the grill. "Who made it?"

"My mom," he answered. "Stereotypical, huh?"

He heard something hit the grill and sizzle. The resulting scent told him it was butter. "No editorializing. Where are you?"

Witt tried to fill in the edges of the memory. "In the kitchen at the ranch house. I'm probably fourteen. I'm in my pajamas so it must have been a sick day from school or something because nobody eats grilled cheese for breakfast."

"You're editorializing again. What's the bread like?"

He dove back into his memory for the details, surprising himself with the ability to recall even the smallest ones. "Crispy around the edges, but soft and white on the inside. It gets butter on my fingers. It gives just the right amount when you bite into it, and then the cheese oozes out everywhere."

"Tell me about the cheese."

"It's got to be that wrapped stuff, 'cause it's alarmingly yellow."

"Editorializing…" she scolded, and he heard the unmistakable sound of her spatula working on the grill. The smell filling the truck was nothing short of amazing.

"Smooth. Melty but just to the right point. It does that stretchy thing when you try to break off a piece, just like the commercials." He was starting to feel ridiculous. "Can I open my eyes now?"

"No. How is it cut? Diagonally or straight across?"

"Is this some sort of Rorschach test? You're going to ask me if I see my childhood trauma in the toast colors or something?"

The spatula banged against the grill. "You

really are impossible, you know that? Just answer the question."

Witt crossed his arms over his chest. The scent was making him hungry. If she was going to make a spectacular grilled cheese sandwich four feet from him and then not let him eat it, she was going to find out what a real argument could be. "Triangles. Mom always said it lets the most cheese ooze out."

"And what does it feel like when you eat it?" Her voice sounded like she had turned to him, although he wasn't quite sure how he knew. His brain seemed to be reaching out for her in multiple directions, which was the most unsettling of sensations.

Searching for the least sappy answer, Witt replied, "Like she knows just how to make something that will make me feel better. Like home and kid stuff."

"And what do you smell now?"

That was easy. "A sandwich I am going to make you let me eat after all this nonsense."

"Bingo," she said, her voice very close. "Open." It took him a split second to realize she was asking him to open his mouth, which felt crazily intimate. He started to open his eyes, needing to drag this experience back into the practical world instead of letting his imagination take over, but she said, "Nope, keep your eyes closed. Here, bite."

He couldn't have refused for all the world. Warm, gooey bliss met his tongue. It was all the things Mom's grilled cheese had been, but not kid stuff—and he couldn't figure out how she'd managed that. The bread was crisp on the outside and soft on the inside but not in a childhood, white-bread kind of way. The cheese wasn't processed, plastic-wrapped squares, but *cheese*—if that made any sense. Texture and flavor and substance and sophistication but still simple. "Mmm," he said, not bothered that he was pretty sure she'd just won the argument they'd been having. Or she'd just cheesed him into concession, which made no sense at all.

She pulled his palm out and flat, and Witt felt her put the paper basket of the sandwich in his outstretched hand. With his eyes closed, the feel of her fingers was wildly heightened, and it sent his pulse up more notches. "Now you can open your eyes," she said, victory in her tone.

He almost didn't want to, convinced it would wreck the moment that was still reverberating under his skin. When he did, she was leaning against the opposite counter, arms crossed over her chest and a smug, catlike smile on her face. The rebellious thought *she's beautiful* popped into his mind and refused to leave. "Point made," she proclaimed as she licked cheese off one finger.

He took another bite. He'd thought her burgers were great, but the woman's grilled cheese could foster world peace. "And what exactly was your point?"

"The *idea* of a grilled cheese is more powerful than any picture. If we put a picture out there, all you will see is a sandwich. If we let the words and the scents do the job, then those mix with your memories and you suddenly want a grilled cheese sandwich."

She was absolutely right. She'd created a fierce craving for grilled cheese—*her* grilled cheese—and hadn't used a single visual. It should feel worse to lose an argument to her. Witt hated losing, hated coming in second to anyone, which was what had made Cole's usurpation especially hard to swallow. What made it so easy to concede to Jana Powers? He'd never had a true partnership with anyone. Sure, he liked working for Gunner and the Blue Thorn, and felt valued, but it was clear who was boss. It should be clear who was boss in this situation, but it wasn't, and he couldn't understand why he didn't mind.

"You're right," he admitted, a little startled by how easily the concession slid off his tongue. For a guy accustomed to digging his heels in, this was new territory. Nice, but definitely foreign. He polished off the first of the four triangles. "This is really good, you know."

"Yes," she replied, her smile a *thank you* rather than an *I won*. "As good as you are at marketing, you could never capture this in a photo. What's going to sell this sandwich is the smell, the idea and the customer in front of you walking away with the cheese dripping off his chin."

She pointed to his chin with a playful look on her face, and his hand went to his lower lip to encounter a glob of warm cheese. He was sitting next to a stack of napkins two feet high, but he stuck his tongue out to catch the bit of cheese and ate it happily. Who knew losing could taste this good?

She'd made a mistake. Watching people eat her cooking—not just consume but really enjoy food that she had prepared—was too much of a thrill for Jana, especially with this man in this tiny space. The energy they'd built up arguing went in an entirely different direction when she fed him the sandwich in this narrow kitchen. The room was warm and close, and it had nothing to do with the Austin sun. She'd retreated to the other side of the truck, but the four feet between them still felt like four inches.

It had been a double-edged sword to ask him to close his eyes. Yes, it had served her purpose of demonstrating the uselessness of visuals to sell cooking, but it had also lent a risky intimacy to the experience. And while it had hid those brilliant blue eyes while she was trying to make her point, it made them all the more striking when he opened them. The look of pleasure and respect in them dropped right through her stomach, so nearly buckling her knees that she was glad she was leaning up against the counter.

She'd won the point, but she was in very real danger of losing her composure. Needing something—anything—to do, she grabbed a spatula and began scraping the leftover brown bits from the sandwich off the grill.

"Want some?" he said, the most endearing half-man-half-boy grin on his face. "I'll share."

Jana shook her head. Even though grilled cheese was one of her favorites, sharing this sandwich with him would just take everything up a notch—or eleven. "I'm glad you like it," she said, thinking it sounded stupid but needing to shove words into the space between them where all this heat was currently lingering.

"Don't tell Mom, but yours is better than hers. Maybe the next truck needs to be Blue Thorn Grilled Cheese." His eyes ignited the way they always did when he got a new idea. "Each truck could have its own specialty, but still offer some common items. The grilled cheese truck could be yellow with blue trim, instead of blue with white trim like this one."

She laughed. "You don't ever shut down, do you?" It was good to get things back on a business tack. His relentless marketing drive annoyed her just enough to douse most of the warmth from their encounter over the sandwich—*most* of it. Jana doubted she'd ever look at a grilled cheese without thinking of him ever again. "We're getting ahead of ourselves. This truck is barely up and running—I don't want to start thinking about expansion just yet. Even if you are thinking about expansion *all the time*."

"That's my job," he said as he polished off the last triangle. "And I do it well. And you, you do your job exceptionally well. You've ruined every other grilled cheese for me. Nothing could measure up to what I just ate."

It ought to feel like hyperbole—Witt was

always putting things in overdone terms—but his eyes were so genuinely pleased she was sure he meant it. *Lord,* she pleaded, *this man needs to stop looking like that when he compliments my cooking.* How could one man push all her buttons in the best and worst ways at the same time? *Please have him say or do something that helps me get myself back under control.*

Witt pulled the truck's tablet off its wall bracket and began tapping away at it. "Is there a blogger who likes grilled cheese? Some celebrity who could give us the equivalent of Elvis Presley's love for the peanut butter and banana sandwich?"

Thank You, Jana prayed, almost glad to feel her annoyance rise. "You are not going to parade my grilled cheese around like a beauty queen. Can we just concentrate on happy customers for now and leave the market share for later?"

He looked up from what she was sure was an internet search for celebrities who love grilled cheese. "Too far?"

This time it wasn't hard to throw him a dark look. "Yes."

One corner of his mouth crept up. "Do you think we'll ever agree on everything? On *anything*?"

"Where'd be the fun in that?" Her answer was close to the truth. Sure, they rarely agreed. But what came out of the mostly respectful disagreements seemed to be the best solutions for everyone.

"I'll let go of the idea of pictures on the menu. And you'll do the interview on *Live at Eight* later this month?"

She'd been so annoyed about the church picnic she'd forgotten all about *Live at Eight*. A television camera crew was coming out to the truck to shoot a segment. There were a dozen reasons why she didn't want to do this, but the fact of the matter was it could be outstanding publicity for the truck. And she'd just won the menu battle, so this seemed like a time to play nice. "Sure. But I want you and Jose there, as well. I want this interview to be about the business and the food, not about me."

"I already asked Jose. We may have to give him an espresso or two—he is a teenage boy after all, and those don't seem to come alive before noon—but he'll be there. And I already told them it was a feature about the food, not the chef. My exact words, actually."

He was trying to meet her halfway. "We're just at the tipping point, Witt, I can feel it. Pretty soon the word of mouth will be strong enough to take over, and we won't have to do much stuff like this anymore. I'm hanging on for that."

He put the tablet back on the wall. "I get that. I really do. And I know you are no fan of the publicity stuff, so…" He stuffed his hands in his pockets, something she'd come to realize he did when he felt out of his depth—which wasn't very often. "I guess I just want to say thank you. You know, for all the PR stunts you've put up with so far. I appreciate that I'm dragging you out of your comfort zone on this. But it will all be worth it in the end. And for what it's worth, I think you really might have fun at the MGCC picnic."

The air in the truck was close and quiet. Jana swallowed as Witt's eyes did that thing that made it hard to say no to the man. The guy had a silver tongue, that was certain, but it was his eyes that truly did the convincing. Buckton blue was an irresistible force. "Okay, fine," she said far more softly than she would have liked.

She wiped her hands on a dish towel, needing somewhere—anywhere—else to look than his eyes. She'd always respected Witt Buckton, but her genuine like for the guy seemed to be expanding beyond her control. She knew, at that moment, that if for some reason he hugged her—a truck victory, a great review, or some social event out at the ranch—she'd let him. She'd hug him back. She never did that kind of thing. Jana hugged her friends, her mom, but never her coworkers. This was dangerous territory. A dynamic way too powerful to cope with in the tiny quarters of the truck.

Needing an excuse to open the door and get outside, she grabbed the half-full trash can and began yanking the plastic garbage bag out of it. Taking out the trash was Jose's job, but right now she needed more air and less Witt. "Okay, so I'll be here at 7:15 like they asked. Jose is coming to wash the truck the night before so she'll be shiny. Shinier."

"Thank you. For all of this," he called.

"You're welcome," she called back, not entirely sure she meant it.

Chapter Seven

Witt looked up from checking the temperature on the meat case the following Tuesday to see his college friend and current roommate, Mark Newman. He didn't care for the dumbstruck look on Mark's face as he stood in the Blue Thorn Store's doorway.

"You're running a yarn shop?" Mark's tone implied he found the pursuit beneath his buddy. Witt was glad Ellie was out to lunch at the moment—she would be on Mark in a heartbeat for a remark like that.

"Do you pay any attention when I talk? I comanage a retail division that happens to have bison yarn as one of its products. Keep the wisecracks about yarn to yourself when my cousin's here, cowboy. She's very proud of her product." He gave Mark a pointed look. "Even prouder than I am of mine."

"I love it when you bring your work home." A big guy with an appetite to match, Mark had never turned down bison burgers when Witt brought some home. "Gotta say, I like that new truck of yours, too. Tasty stuff." Mark walked farther into the store. "And the view's not too shabby, either. Where'd you find the girl chef?"

The girl chef. Witt had used those exact words weeks ago, but now they grated on his nerves. "Ellie knew her from her old job in Atlanta. And she's not a 'girl chef,' Mark, she's a chef. Period." Some part of Witt wanted to growl *off-limits, buddy* to his friend, but he swallowed the warning. Despite his occasional lack of tact, Mark was a stand-up guy and a loyal friend. It's not as if he was some jerk who would break Jana's heart. Besides, Witt had no jurisdiction whatsoever over Jana's social life, and short of it just feeling weird, Witt had no valid reason to warn Mark off. After all, if Jana liked people who appreciated her cooking, few people liked eating more than Mark. The guy put away enough food for three people.

"She's a good chef. Been back twice since you opened up. I usually eat Mexican before a gig, but I've decided a Blue Thorn burger may be just the preperformance protein this body needs."

"You play bass, Mark, not football. I'm not sure protein consumption or carbo-loading really comes into it." Witt adopted the stereotypical bass-player pose—one hip cocked out, low-slung guitar, head bobbing to imaginary music. "Not really an athletic pursuit, you know?"

Mark feigned insult. "I expend a lot of energy on stage. I put it all out there for my fans."

Witt slid the case doors shut. "All three of them."

"Hey, we're playing some big food festival thing later this month. It's a contest thing for food trucks. You should totally enter. I think there's prize money, even."

"We're not ready for that. Jana's very particular about her food service. She wants us to have everything perfect before we start drawing lots of attention to ourselves. I don't think I'd get her to enter something like a contest for at least two months."

"Well, you can just come see the band, then. Scope out your competition. Maybe bring Miss Chef with you so she can hear us, too."

"She'll hear you at the picnic, remember? The truck is catering and your band is playing."

"And maybe she'll come in here and see my magnetic smile while I'm working, right?"

Witt had asked Mark to stop by to talk about working a few days a week here at the store. He was starting to rethink the choice.

Mark caught on to his friend's hesitation. "Or not. I don't want to muddy the waters between you and your star employee." He set down the backpack he was carrying. "Do you want things to go beyond professional between you two? I mean, look at her. You'd have to be dead not to have at least considered it."

That was Mark, never holding back. "No," Witt insisted, "I have not considered it." *Much.* Because there's nothing to consider. We work together, Mark. It'd be the worst idea, ever. We get along—well, half of the time, that is, since she's got no shortage of opinions on everything—but our relationship is purely business related. No way would I risk anything as unprofessional as dating my chef."

"You're right. You're smarter than that. Sorry I brought it up." He pressed his hand down on the meat scale, watching the numbers register the weight. "So tell me what you need me to do. Two days a week, right?"

Witt was glad to shift to a safer topic. "Just for the next month. After that, I won't have to be at the truck so much. I'm thinking Tuesdays and Thursdays."

"Am I going to have to sell yarn?" Mark looked less than thrilled at the prospect.

"You said you can work a cash register, right?"

"Yeah."

"Well, the price tag's right there on the yarn and the knitted goods. You ring them up same as a steak or a box of burgers." He peeled Mark's hand off the scale. "It's even easier than that, since you don't have to weigh anything like you do some of the *meat*." He emphasized the last word, hoping to imply the scale was not a toy.

Mark shifted to stand behind the cash register. "Looks easy enough to me." For the next twenty minutes, Witt showed him the particulars of weighing out steaks and ground bison meat, calculating the price and wrapping for sale. It wasn't rocket science, and Mark was a smart guy.

"Your sister called the apartment," Mark slipped in casually halfway through the demonstration. "She said she left a message on your cell."

"She did. I've been swamped this morning."

Mark sat back against the rear counter, a doubtful look filling his features. "She said it's her third message. Come on, you've got to mend that fence sometime. Mary's your sister. She was asking me all about the truck thing. She's excited for you."

She's glad I've taken myself out of the equation, Witt thought darkly, even though he knew it wasn't true. Mary was stuck in the middle of their father's difficult decision, torn between pride at her husband's clear success and empathy at her brother's pain over being usurped. "I'll mend it." *I ought to*, Witt thought to himself. *I know You'd want me to, Lord, but I am just not ready.*

"When?" Mark persisted. That was the blessing and the curse of friendship with Mark—nothing ever went unsaid with the guy. "Don't you think this whole mess has gone on long enough? You made your choice, and it's a good one. I was glad to move up here with you—the music scene is fabulous in Austin, and you would never have been happy staying down in San Antonio, playing second fiddle to Cole. But that doesn't mean you can just ignore your family. She's your sister."

"Can we just drop the subject for now?" Witt pulled open a desk drawer and retrieved the paperwork Mark had to fill out. "I've got a full plate getting the truck up and running, and you know how much I need this to succeed. When things get settled, I'll patch things up with them, but I could use the distance right now."

"I get it," Mark replied, "but you've got to at least return phone calls. It's harsh not to."

"I'll send her a text," Witt conceded.

Mark picked up Witt's cell phone from off the desk and handed it to him. "Good."

"Right now?"

Mark crossed his hands over his chest. "She told me she was planning to drive up to Austin this week. She wanted to know where the truck's going to be."

She'd left a message to that effect on his cell. It was part of the reason Witt hadn't called her back. He knew his sister genuinely wanted to be supportive, but he hated the tone he heard whenever his San Antonio family talked about the food truck. As if it was a trendy little gimmick rather than a real business.

Mark caught Witt's expression. "Tell her

where the truck will be. Let her come show you some support. You've got the chance to smooth this over, so don't be an idiot. Take it." After a pause, Mark added, "I'm not leaving here until you text her. Honestly, man, you're as stubborn as your dad."

That did it. Making an effort to wipe the scowl from his face, Witt pulled up the contact for his sister and began typing in a message. Mark was right. Mary was putting in an effort, and the least he could do was meet her halfway.

The night before the church picnic, Jana couldn't sleep. Feeding a line of customers one at a time was one thing—providing dinner to a whole congregation was quite another. And not just any congregation, but one that clearly meant a lot to Witt, Gunner, Ellie and their grandmother. The pressure kept her tossing and turning in bed until she finally pulled on a pair of jeans and T-shirt and went out into the truck at 3:00 a.m. If she couldn't get the sleep that eluded her, perhaps she'd get a leg up on the challenge with extra preparations. Well, that and a lot of coffee.

Yawning, Jana pulled open the truck door and snapped on the light. It pleased her how much the truck felt like home by now, a quiet little haven, even in the middle of the night. Her kitchen.

Jana found a box sitting on the counter. A square gift box, wrapped in bright blue ribbon. She saw an envelope tucked under the ribbon, with "Jana" written in what she recognized as Witt's bold handwriting. Pulling the stool out from under the counter, Jana set down her travel mug of extra strong coffee and opened the envelope.

Jana—
The Blue Thorn Ranch has a tradition that's gone on for four generations. Each and every hand, every family member, every person who lends their efforts to make the Blue Thorn thrive, wears a turquoise bandanna. It's how we mark our own, a way to let each person know they belong.

You should have had these from the first day. There's a dozen in this box, because you should wear one every day and I know they'll get dirty. They're supposed to—we all sweat and strive to keep the Blue Thorn up and running.

I'm sorry I didn't think of it before now. You may be in a truck forty miles from the Blue Thorn, but you are as

much a part of it as any of us. And I'm
glad you are.
—Witt
PS, There are two for Jose, as well.

Jana swallowed hard, the lump in her throat
and the fatigue in her bones bringing her
close to tears. She was part of something. A
vital part. The place in her heart that had felt
ignored or dismissed for so long seemed to
come back to life, to feel free and alive instead of boxed in and surviving. She was infi-
nitely glad Witt had known to leave her alone
with the gift—she couldn't bear the thought
of welling up like this in front of him. She
wasn't ready for anyone—much less Witt—
to see that side of her.

Jana lifted the lid on the box and held up
the bright blue square with its intricate black-
and-white paisley-like markings. Yes, it was
just a swatch of cloth, but it was also so much
more. It was a mark of belonging, and up
until this moment, Jana hadn't realized how
much she'd felt as if she no longer belonged
anywhere.

Slowly, gratefully, she folded the square,
gathered up her hair and pulled it back using

the bandanna as a headband. It felt…well, what other word was there for a chef to use? It felt delicious.

Chapter Eight

The following weekend, Jana watched the man everyone called Pastor Theo walk up to the truck with a wide smile on his face. "I can't thank you enough for this. Our All Saints' Day picnic is usually a potluck affair—and I love a good potluck—but this ups the game in a whole new way."

"Thank the Bucktons," Jana replied as she put another load of potatoes into the fryer. "They're the ones who made this happen."

"Well, you volunteered your time, as well. They bought the provisions, but you cooked them. I confess I've had a bison burger before, but not like yours. And people haven't stopped talking about your coleslaw."

"That's always nice to hear." Jana gave the minister a smile. Despite her reservations, she'd found she enjoyed and needed the slew of compliments she'd received tonight. Everyone was so supportive and friendly. Even with the signifying bandanna in her pocket, that felt like foreign territory. "Tell everyone to tell all their friends," she reminded the pastor.

Theo laughed. "I don't think I'll need to remind them. I think Blue Thorn Burgers made a lot of new fans tonight." He took another step toward the counter. "And I hope I can say Martins Gap Community Church has made a new friend."

"Who, me?"

"Of course. And not just behind the grill. You're welcome in the pews. Or even in the choir, for that matter." He leaned in. "I'm not entirely sure singing talent is a requirement."

Jana laughed. "Well, it sure looks like a friendly enough place."

"Witt tells me you go to church in Austin."

She didn't know quite what to make of the fact that Witt had been talking to Pastor Theo about her. Then again, it may have just been during the setup for today's event. "I do. The Awakenings congregation. They meet in an old warehouse down on South Congress. The services are a bit rock 'n' roll for your crowd, I'd expect."

"Oh, we're not so down-home country that we can't appreciate a good drum beat,"

Theo replied. "I'm fixing to launch a Saturday night service for the young people one of these days. Maybe even with Mark's band." He put his hands in his pockets. "You know, if we included food service, I imagine we'd pack 'em in."

For a small-town country pastor, Jana liked this guy's out-of-the-box thinking. "We'll be down in Austin most Saturday nights, Pastor."

"Theo," the reverend corrected. "Just Theo is fine."

"Theo," she revised. "So I don't think we can help out. But you might have the same results with Shorty's Pizza."

"Pizza would get me here. Even Shorty's," Jose offered. Jana had discovered the teen to be exceedingly picky about his food. He had a chef's palate, to be sure—a far cry from the usual teenage eat-anything-in-sight appetite.

"I'll give it some thought," Theo said, smiling.

"Give what some thought?" Witt came up behind the pastor.

"Saturday-night church with Shorty's Pizza," Jana offered as she slid another half dozen burgers onto a tray Jose was shuttling out to the tables.

"Is Martins Gap ready for so radical an idea?" Witt posed.

"You reach people where they are, Witt, not where you want them to be." He patted his stomach. "And I've always found food to be a great welcomer." With that, another member of the congregation called to him and the pastor walked away with a wave.

"I like him," Jana offered as Witt climbed up into the truck.

"Theo? He's a good guy. He's done a lot for this town, and made a lot happen for the folks who live here. Solid man, good preacher—" Witt leaned in "—but a terrible speller. If it weren't for his secretary, Dottie, he'd be in deep trouble I'm told."

Somehow that made Jana like the guy all the more. "We all have our weaknesses."

"My new weakness is your grilled cheese. I haven't eaten all night." He leaned casually up against the truck's back wall, an engaging smile lighting up those dazzling blue eyes. "Care to indulge me, Chef?"

Jana grabbed the bread from the cabinet under the grill. "Sure thing, boss." Of course she'd make him one; he was her boss, after all. But that smile brought back the memory of the last time she'd made him a grilled cheese. Things had sizzled between them—

and she wasn't talking about the sandwich—and the thought of it made her stomach flip just a bit. She reached down and fingered the cloth square in her chef's coat pocket—as she had a dozen times this afternoon—and remembered the surprisingly tender words he had written on the card with the bandannas. They hadn't spoken about it, yet. She wasn't ready to—not in the midst of all the preceding chaos.

"This was fun, wasn't it?" Witt asked. "I mean, it wasn't too much work for you and Jose?"

"No, it was fine. You were right—everyone was really nice. It's good to remember what a pleasure it can be to cook for people who appreciate it."

"Oh, they definitely appreciate it. You're a hit."

"Blue Thorn Burgers is a hit," she corrected as she turned the bread and carefully laid the cheese on top.

"Sure, but it's more than that. You connect to people. They like you, and they feel how much you like them. Whatever that is, I don't have it."

Jana highly doubted that. She found him a lot more compelling than was wise. Did he truly not realize how charismatic he was, or was he just playing at humility? She studied him as she finished cooking the sandwich, and decided his father's rejection had done serious damage. Witt Buckton seemed to feel like he had to prove himself, but she didn't see why. He was clearly his own man—why couldn't he see that for the strength it was?

"What?" Witt asked.

She'd been staring, almost allowing the sandwich to burn. "Nothing," she covered, forcing her gaze back down to the grill.

Witt stood up. "You need to get out from behind this grill and have a bit of fun. Is Jose ready to make a few burgers?"

As a matter of fact, this was a safe place to let her protégé stretch his wings. Jose had begged her to let him make a few burgers the other day, and he'd done a passable job. Not much flair yet, but he had the basic techniques down and watched her every chance he could. "I think we can let him handle the next dozen."

"Come on, then. Mark's band just played their final set and they're about to start the gutter sundae."

"The what?"

"The huge long ice cream sundae. You like ice cream, don't you?"

Of course she did. Who didn't? "Your sandwich?"

He pointed down to the grill. "I think it's past its prime."

Jana looked down to see the cheese and crusts blackened and smoking. "What?" She hadn't burned anything she'd cooked in nearly two years. This guy was really getting to her. Was the black-edged bread a metaphor for the danger of what buzzed between them, or just a signal of how distractible she was around him?

Witt shrugged. "Ice cream is a good plan B." Jose was coming up the back entrance of the truck, an empty tray in his hands. "Hey, Jose, want to take over for a few minutes?"

"Me? Really?"

Jana smiled and handed him the spatula—but not before scooping up the ruined grilled cheese and sliding it into the garbage can. "You're ready. And this is an easy crowd."

Jose grinned and took the spatula. "Yes, Chef!"

"I'm impressed," Witt commented as he led Jana to the part of the church lawn where a long white gutter had been propped up on sawhorses. Gran had always invited him and Mary up for the church picnic, and gutter sundae was one of his favorite parts. He was pleased they still did it, and pleased to be able to show Jana the crazy event.

"At what? I burned the sandwich." Her brows knit together. "Do you know how long it's been since I've burned anything?"

He filed that away in the back of his mind—the part that was intrigued by how completely distracted he could make her. The part that wondered why she wasn't wearing one of the blue bandannas he'd left for her. Jana hadn't even mentioned the gift. Did she not want to be considered part of the Blue Thorn family? She deserved to wear their trademark bandanna. And, when he was completely honest with himself, he wanted her to wear it. When it had to do with her, he was coming to want a lot of things that were bad for business.

"I'm impressed you let Jose take over, even for ten minutes," he continued. "You're a bit of a tyrant in your own kitchen, you know." He made sure his tone was warm and his smile was wide when he said that. He couldn't explain why he found her total commitment to cooking endearing—most times it only made things more complicated and difficult—but he could also recognize that it was what made Jana the chef she was.

Jana looked back over her shoulder at the truck. "Yeah, well…"

"Relax, he'll be fine. You've been training him well, he has a natural knack for it and this is a very forgiving crowd. Don't forget, Jose comes from Martins Gap. Folk know him and love him here." He directed Jana's attention to the spectacle in front of them. "And I'd hate for you to miss this."

Witt watched her stare at the long white object, waiting for her to work out what it was. "That's a rain gutter. Like from a house."

"Brand-new and washed up squeaky clean, but yes."

Her eyes followed the gutter until it met the team of men depositing dozens of scoops of ice cream into the makeshift "dish." He'd eaten a gutter sundae for so many years that he'd gotten used to the oddity. It was fun to watch her take the crazy tradition in for the first time. She glanced up at Witt, amusement and amazement filling her eyes. "You've got to be kidding me."

"Every picnic. The hardware store donates a longer and longer gutter each year, I think. Here comes the next part." Witt pointed to the four-person sauce team—two chocolate, two caramel—who followed along behind the ice cream brigade. "Takes quick work to get it all done in this heat. Come on."

Jana made a delightful squeak of surprise as he took her elbow and pulled her to the crate of whipped cream cans. "This is an honor, so enjoy it." With that, Witt popped the top off four cans, handing two to her and taking two himself. "Knock yourself out."

She hesitated for just a moment as he stood at the ready across her on the other side of the gutter. Then she attacked. He'd planned to use one can at a time, but Jana had already worked out how to use two at once to go twice as fast, a technique he adopted as soon as he could. By halfway through the cans, Jana was giggling. When someone thrust two more cans into her hands at the end of the first set, she was laughing outright, and it had become an all-out race between them to see who would get to the end of this set of canisters. Cheers rose up behind them, and something electric buzzed in his chest when he caught her eye. The moment was a perfect mix of play and competition, miles away from their professional dynamic.

Four cans later, she reached the end of the gutter first, and proclaimed her victory with a squirt right at Witt. He wiped the frothy goodness off his chin with the back of his hand and then licked it clean, not one bit annoyed that he'd been bested. He simply returned fire. When Jana reached into her pocket to produce the blue bandanna and wipe off her spattered face with the most extraordinary sparkle in her eyes, Witt's stomach dropped out through the soles of his boots.

Without a word, he gave her a wide, warm grin and handed her a long plastic spoon. The last two teams—nuts and cherries—met them at the end. Witt held Jana's gaze as he raised the spoon. When Pastor Theo rang the church bell, he, Jana and every other member of the congregation dug in.

It was just ice cream and toppings—he knew that—but the silly dessert tradition had always been a favorite of his, one he was delighted to share with her. The fact that she seemed to enjoy it as much as he did, that it finally let out the playful side he was sure lived under all that serious cooking, that she had indeed kept the bandanna close, well, that just added to the charm.

"Wow," she said, licking her spoon clean when only melted remains pooled in the bottom of the gutter. "That's…I actually don't have a word for what that was." She had chocolate sauce on her bottom lip, and Witt ignored the crazy urge to reach out and wipe it off. Instead, he pointed to her lip and handed her a napkin from a nearby table.

It made his spine tingle when she used the bandanna again instead. "Fun, crazy, delicious?" he suggested.

Several people came up to Jana and complimented her on her fast flourish with a whipped cream can. Audie, Gunner's stepdaughter, came up with a huge grin. "Uncle Nash says he might need to deputize you when he takes over as sheriff soon." She giggled.

"I doubt that," Witt said, glancing over at his cousin and her fiancé. Nash had just been elected to take over when the current sheriff retired later this month. Nash and Ellie had a grand new life ahead of them, and looked just as love-struck as any soon-to-be newlyweds ought to look. *I want that someday,* Witt thought to himself. He tried not to let his mind wander to Jana. He'd never dated anyone he worked with, and now certainly wasn't the time to start. He wasn't even sure now was a good time to for him to try to start a relationship with anyone. Their plates were full enough as it was getting the truck established—an emotional entanglement, especially with someone as high-charged as Jana, could spell doom. Still, that didn't mean they couldn't be friends and enjoy a fun church picnic. Work hard, play hard, right?

Jana cleared her throat, and Witt realized he'd been staring. She adjusted her ponytail and straightened her chef's coat. "I'd better get back to the truck," she said, the playfulness replaced by a cautious wonder. "I can't leave Jose unsupervised for long, after all."

Witt looked back at the truck. "Hasn't burned it down yet," he joked. "The gutter sundae marks the official end of dinner, anyway."

"So, time to clean up." The all-business edge to her voice hadn't entirely returned— her face and tone were a little softer than before. And he'd seen her laugh and be silly. She had a blue bandanna in her pocket. That ought to be enough for one night. They had a business to build, after all.

Chapter Nine

The past two days had gone exceptionally well. Tomorrow would mark the one-month anniversary of her meeting Witt that first morning at the bright blue truck, and things were running mostly how she'd hoped they would. Many of the processes had been ironed out to a smooth pace. They'd been to their third location of the day today, and at each spot they were greeted by a small crowd of expectant, hungry customers.

Jana felt herself settling into the rhythm of things. She could give commands to Jose with only one or two words now, and they worked in a coordinated kind of frenzy that made Jana's heart sing. She'd been waiting for that point where the craziness of the kitchen was about logistics, not fear. That wondrous moment where her doubts about the quality of the food or the makeup of the menu faded away, and the only driving force was how to feed waiting customers.

As she slid another four sets of burgers onto the grill, Jana looked out over the line. Seven deep, but not a single one of them was checking their watch or looking around to see if a quicker meal was to be had elsewhere. Witt had been right—six wasn't too long a line.

In the past month, he'd been right about a lot of things. Their minor squabbles had all but disappeared as each of them learned what fights to pick and which points to concede. It really had become the partnership she'd hoped it would be. Jana found herself turning the ignition key each morning filled with excitement for the day ahead.

Witt was in the truck today. He wasn't always anymore—he would usually stop by during the lunch rush, but generally only stayed a long time on Tuesdays or Thursdays. While she always enjoyed his company—well, almost always, for they still had what he continued to call "spirited debates" and she termed arguments—Jana found she didn't need him on-site all the time. Their confidence in each other had grown over the past few weeks, so that she knew when he wasn't there, he was out bolstering the business for the truck or the ranch in other ways. And she knew he trusted her to do everything that needed to be done here.

She admitted—if only to herself—that she liked the days when he hung around. This afternoon he was leaning in the open door, watching the customers receive their food. Then Jana saw it: out of the corner of her eye she watched Witt's entire body language change. He stiffened, his eyes narrowed and his hands stuffed into his pockets. Shifting a few sliders to another part of the grill, she followed his gaze out to where it landed on a couple at the back of the line.

The woman had a slender build with Witt's brownish hair and blue eyes so striking that Jana could see them from the grill. Buckton blue eyes. She pointed at something, offering a smiling comment to her companion, a tall, charismatic guy with dark features. They weren't wearing the delighted expectation she could see on other customers' faces. It took her a minute to work out exactly what it was she saw in their faces, distracted as she was by the burgers in front of her and Witt's bristling off to her right. As she handed a set of sliders to Jose to ring up, her stomach dropped and she identified the couple's attitude: amusement. And not necessarily the good kind—no, this was closer to the condescending, "bless her heart" kind of tolerance of which Southern women were skilled masters.

That could only mean one thing: Mary and Cole Sullivan, Witt's sister and bother-in-law, were here to eat Blue Thorn Burgers. *Oh, boy.*

Was that a good thing? Casting a glance back at Witt, Jana could hardly tell. All the confidence she'd felt just moments before seeped out through the bottoms of her shoes. Mary and Cole clearly weren't expecting to be impressed, even though Jana knew her burgers could impress anyone. She counted five customers before them—that gave her a bit of time to gather her thoughts.

Witt had clearly seen the couple, but had they seen Witt? Jana kept waiting for him to step down out of the truck and go greet them, but he didn't move. He slid his hands back out of his pockets, but very slowly. As if he were commanding himself to hold back.

Was she supposed to know who they were? Should she greet them? Treat them like any other customer? She tried to catch Witt's eyes, but in the bustle of orders she couldn't get his attention. No, his focus was laser-sharp and exclusively on the very nicely dressed couple working their way to the front of the line.

"Witt," she called when they were three customers away. She needed direction from him, because this looked like it could go twelve different ways—some of them decidedly unpleasant. Jana was glad she didn't have to say more than just his name—as soon as he turned to face her, Witt's eyes told her he knew she'd guessed who they were. He gave her a look that silently translated—she hoped—to "just serve them like everybody else" as he stepped down out of the truck.

Jana was just wondering what to do when Witt's sister made the opening gesture. "You must be Jana," the woman called as she stepped up to the window. She didn't bother with Jose at the cash register, but stood right in front of Jana.

"I am," Jana said as brightly as she could. "What'll it be?"

"My brother, Witt, says the sliders are terrific."

So it *was* Mary—not that she'd really doubted it. Which meant that must be Cole. If Texas had a stereotypical power couple, she had a feeling she was looking at it. It was clear not just in the way they dressed, but in the way they held themselves that these were people accustomed to and comfortable with being in charge. Jana fought the urge to straighten her hair in light of the stunningly perfect couple in front of her. They did not look like the usual food truck burger demographic, that's for sure. "They are," she said with confidence she didn't feel. "You must be Mary," she added, only because it felt like the polite thing to do. "And Cole. Nice to meet you. I'd shake your hands, but…"

"I get it," Cole said, flashing a wide smile. "The deluxe meal with the slaw for me. And two iced teas. Unsweetened."

"Coming right up," Jana said as she accepted an order ticket from Jose, who'd been scribbling as they talked.

"That'll be…" Jose said punching cash register buttons as Cole took his wallet from his pants pocket.

"On the house," Jana cut in, making a split-second decision. Then, amending her impulse, she added, "Just this once," with a friendly smile.

Mary laughed. "Does Witt know you're giving away food?"

Witt appeared from out of nowhere to stand on Mary's other side. "She did say just this once." There was a hint of ice in his voice, something Jana could never remember hearing from Witt. Even Jose shot her a sideways glance as he handed Cole the two drinks and moved on to the next customers.

For the next ten minutes, Jana's mind spun in multiple directions. She focused on Mary's and Cole's orders, wanting them to be perfect because it was clear Witt felt judged by their presence. She kept up the string of orders that followed because lines, just as Witt had convinced her, were some of the best publicity Blue Thorn Burgers could have. Adding cheese to one burger, she threw up a blurt of thankful prayer that Mary and Cole had seen the truck today, when it was at its best. If they had come on one of those first fumbling days, she knew Witt would have taken it worse than any ding Spatula Dave could sling at them. Every chance she could, she cast a glance over to Witt, his sister and her husband as they sat at a picnic table with their food. Did they like it? Were they here to show support? Had Witt invited them or had another family member tipped them off to the truck's location? Had she done the wrong thing by comping their food? It had seemed like a natural choice to make—something she would do when Mom came from Atlanta and showed up at the truck. But Mom would come to cheer, not to judge.

Finally, after about thirty minutes, there

was a break in the rush. Jana wiped her brow, straightened up around the kitchen and dug into her handbag for a comb and a bit of blush. If Witt was going to bring that dapper pair back to the truck after their meal, she wanted to look better than a sweaty fry cook. She knew her tension made no sense from a practical standpoint. Did it really matter what Mary and Cole thought of her or her food? They had no stake in how well Blue Thorn Burgers or even how the whole Blue Thorn Ranch fared. But she felt the need to ensure that the truck, the truck's food and the truck's chef made a good impression, for Witt's sake.

Witt returned alone after saying a stiff goodbye—*Not even a hug,* Jana thought to herself—just a few forced waves. He'd said that Mary and he were close once, but today showed Jana just how deep the wound of Cole's installment—and the subsequent downsizing of Witt's role at Star Beef—had cut. What father would hurt his own son like that? What success was worth the estrangement she just saw play out right in front of her? *I don't have siblings*, she told herself as Witt climbed into the truck, his face set tight. *I can't really understand how all this works*. But she ached for Witt, all the same.

Jana waited for him to talk about the encounter, but he stayed silent, staring at some paper Mary must have given him. Rather than pry, she began washing some lettuce while Jose refilled the napkin containers. That's why his question a few minutes later startled her.

"Why'd you do that?"

"Do what?" Witt watched Jana reply to his question with cautious eyes.

"Give them their food free. Why'd you do that?" Witt knew he'd given Jana authority to comp any meal she chose. This wasn't a procedural question.

She busied herself with a colander of lettuce before she looked at him. "Why was I nice to your *sister*, you mean?" She gave the word emphasis, as if *sister* explained everything.

It bugged him she could be so magnanimous to Mary and Cole. "They can easily afford to pay." The words sounded weak and petty as he spoke them, and he wanted to take them back, but was too irritated to try.

"Oh, I could see that." She gave him the kind of glare she gave Jose when he spent too much time chatting up girls in line. A disappointed "you should know better" slow burn of deep brown eyes. "Fancy couple, those two." She gave the colander a firm shake and then dumped the leaves out onto a towel. "I did it to be nice. They're your family. I would have comped my mom or Jose's brother if they'd showed up." Jose's brother had shown up, twice, but she'd never mentioned her mom making an appearance. If Mrs. Powers had made the trip from Atlanta, it bothered him that he hadn't been introduced. Then again, he'd not gone out of his way to have Jana come say a more extended hello to Mary and Cole, even when the line had died down. Family was so complicated and annoying and painful.

"That wasn't a show of familial support, if that's what you're implying," he told her. Rather than risk another look at Jana, he stared out the window at the picnic table where they had been sitting. A young family had taken up the spot, dad clearly settling mom and toddler in the pleasant shade while he came up to the truck to order. Witt thought about the little stuffed bison made out of bison yarn that Ellie made to give kids when they came to visit the ranch and wondered if he should stock a few in the truck. *Sure, give away toys but skimp on your own sister*, he scolded himself. Mary could get under his skin in a heartbeat since Cole took over, and Witt could barely be civil to his new brother-in-law.

Jana planted a defiant hand on one hip. "Oh, I get that they were here to check you out. All the more reason to be nice, if you ask me. Be the better man and all."

"Take the high road," Jose offered until both of them shot the boy a look. "Why don't I go check on the chalkboard?" He shot from the truck muttering something containing the word *familia*. Smart kid to see a storm coming and get out of the way—the truck was a claustrophobic space to have an argument, and Witt felt one brewing. He always felt one brewing when it came to Mary these days. Why had he let Mark talk him into including Mary's email in the truck's location announcement list?

"Didn't you expect them to show up one of these days?" she asked cautiously while she busied herself with the lettuce.

"Hadn't really thought about it, actually." *That's not true*, Witt thought to himself. *You know you as much as handed her an invitation when you added her to the list to get those emails*. Witt put the paper down on top of the zippered leather folder he used as a daily briefcase of sorts. Bison leather, of course, monogrammed with his initials. A "welcome to the company" gift from Gunner, and far nicer than the "traitor" look Dad had given him when he'd announced his installment as vice president of Blue Thorn Enterprises. "I try not to think too much about Mary and Cole these days. Things haven't exactly cooled off between us, as you can see."

"Oh, I don't know. That exchange looked pretty icy to me." She paused for a moment before venturing, "Are things really that bad between you?"

She said it as if the friction was avoidable. As if there was a graceful way to swallow his ousting at the hands of Cole's non-Buckton charisma. If there was, he sure hadn't found it. He chose not to reply, flicking through a sanitation checklist hung on a clipboard near the back door. He didn't need to check it—he knew everything would be in perfect order. The truck was running far above his expectations, growing faster in this past month than even his optimistic goals had predicted. He owed a lot of that to the woman in front of him, which meant he owed her better treatment than making her bear the brunt of his bad mood after this latest clash of overgrown sibling rivalry.

She tried again. "Let me guess. They were impressed, but they made good and sure they were condescending about how they showed it. Honestly, it looked like Cole was going to reach out and pat you on the head or put a smiley face and 'Good job!' on your food truck worksheet."

Jana was teasing him—he knew that—but she struck so close to home he didn't know how to reply. Could she read him that easily? Or were Cole and Mary just that obvious in their sense of unbridled superiority? Witt replaced the clipboard to its spot on the wall and just grunted. "He gets to me. I know Mary loves him, and they make a good couple, but he just…gets to me. And honestly, when she's with him, she's not much better. She can't just be happy for me—it has to come wrapped up in a patronizing attitude."

Jana leaned up against the counter, eyes understanding rather than judgmental. "So don't let them get to you. Sure, he blocked your path in one way—in a really big way, if you ask me—but you found another. One you're really good at. You wouldn't be here launching us if things hadn't happened the way they did. That's where the faith part comes in, right?"

Despite being at a church picnic together a few days ago, he and Jana had never deeply talked about faith. He knew she went to church, and she obviously knew about his church, but it wasn't like they went to church together. She had her congregation here in Austin, and he had Martins Gap Community Church.

Jana was right; he had to have faith that God's hands had shaped all the events for the best. Part of him knew that to be the truth. He *was* happy launching Blue Thorn Burgers—much happier than he could ever really remember being back at Star Beef—but the sting hadn't gone away. "On my good days, I know that," he offered, trying to smile.

"On my good days, I know Spatula Dave is probably some guy who lives in his mother's basement and trashes restaurants to feel a sense of power."

Witt laughed. "That's exactly the kind of crack I would have made to make you feel better."

Jana held up a scolding finger to her spatula, shaking it as if she were giving Spatula Dave a piece of her mind. "So I won't let Dave get to me if you don't let Cole get to you." She looked at him. "Deal?"

If Witt were going to think about God's hand in all this, one of these days he was going to have to give some serious thanks for the amazing woman God had sent to be his partner in this crazy scheme. "Deal," he said, feeling some of the tension slough off his shoulders.

Jana pointed to the paper with the spatula. "What's that?"

Okay, maybe it was a good time to talk about that paper—and the information it held about the Austin food truck contest. When Mark had posed the idea of them entering their truck, Witt had dismissed it immediately. When he'd come in the truck, he'd considered himself too rankled to consider the idea, but this was his partner, right? They ought to talk about it. "Something Mark mentioned earlier. Cole just gave me a paper with the info on it, too." Witt was glad he was too sure of his friendship with Mark to suspect Mark had tipped Cole off. No, this felt just like the kind of gauntlet Cole would throw down all on his own.

His scowl at the sheet of paper drew a raised eyebrow from her. "And it's still in one piece?"

Did she think him so petulant that he'd even shred a good idea if it came from his brother-in-law? "It might be a good idea, actually." When she gave him a look, he added, "Yes, I get it, even my dastardly brother-in-law can give me a good idea. Well, that and the fact that Mark thought of it, as well."

"Dastardly? Spend a lot of time thinking up adjectives for your brother-in-law, do you?"

He liked when she teased him. It never cut or condemned; it was always funny and supportive even when it came with a "you know better" attitude—like now. "Do you want to hear the good idea or not?"

She looked out the window, checking to see that no other customers needed service, then pulled the little stainless-steel stool out from under the counter. That proved she was going to really listen to him, which gave Witt further inducement to float the idea. Ten minutes ago, he was sure she'd nix it, but now he thought he might stand a chance.

"The Austin Convention and Visitors Bureau is sponsoring a food truck rodeo. It's a..."

Her eyes darkened. "I know what it is."

"Normally, I'd say we're not ready. Only I think we are."

Jana shook her head. "We have no shot at winning a food contest."

"Don't you sell us short. Even if we don't win, I think we'd make a decent showing. It'd be far more publicity that we could ever afford on our own. Placing second or third would get our name—and your name—out there fast."

"Don't you think we're already growing fast enough?"

"We are, but this could make a lot of things possible, even if we only make the finals. If even Cole thinks we're ready…"

She sat back. "Oh, so *that's* what this is about. Aren't you a little old to fall for 'I dare you's?'"

Witt's jaw wanted to bite down on something. Hard. "Oh, so a twenty-five-thousand-dollar grant and a business loan to expand isn't anything we could use? We could open a second truck and even skip straight to the restaurant with that kind of backing. You're ready to pass this up because you think I'm only interested since Cole's egging me on?"

He saw the same surprise on her face that he'd felt when Cole had handed him the paper. Mark hadn't mentioned the size of the first-place prize, and this was no small-potatoes incentive. Winning this would catapult Blue Thorn Burgers into success faster than anything he or Jana could ever do. It wasn't just highly attractive, it was downright irresistible. He handed her the sheet outlining the contest.

"We can't win this," she said after scanning it for a moment.

"I think you have a real shot," he countered. "I think you're that good."

"The prize money is only for first place, and we'll never take that. We're not ready."

"I think we are," he countered, surprised at how fast he'd embraced the challenge. "Will you at least think about it?"

"Maybe." The tone of her one word sounded much closer to *no*.

He could make an executive decision and declare that they were entering. He was the boss, after all. But Witt wanted Jana to embrace the idea before going forward. The look currently on her face, however, gave very little hope for that.

Chapter Ten

Witt handed Jose his paycheck. Most adults Witt knew took something like a paycheck for granted, but Jose always cracked a million-dollar smile when he accepted his. He'd grown fond of the dark-eyed, messy-haired, energetic kid since hiring him on, and wanted to let him know that he was appreciated. "You're doing great work, Jose."

Jose folded the envelope and tucked it in the back pocket of his jeans. "Thanks, boss."

Thursday morning was restocking day, and Jana had gone off to meet a potential new vendor just down the street, leaving Jose to do some deep cleaning and restock paper goods. Witt leaned up against the vehicle with a cup of coffee. "Do you like it here? Working at the truck?"

"You kidding? I love it here." Jose leaned

against the truck with the coffee Witt had brought him along with the paycheck. The boy stuffed his free hand in his pocket and crossed one big foot over the other. He wore baggy jeans and an outrageous but scuffed-up pair of cowboy boots, yet somehow managed to never look scraggly. Wild, yes, but never unkempt. Jose was a creative, vibrant character—*the perfect chef persona*, Jana had said.

"The food, the social media stuff, learning to cook—this is the greatest. I don't even mind taking out the garbage here, and I hate doing that at home."

"You don't miss home? Your buddies in Martins Gap?" Jose lived with his brother here in Austin while he worked on the truck, but Witt had wondered if the separation from his friends and the rest of his family had been working out okay.

Jose shrugged. "I still see plenty of them. Mateo and I go back about once a week, more if we have time. We can still talk, text. If I had found a job in Martins Gap, I'd still be at work all day, so it's not like they really see that much less of me." He offered Witt a look. "You don't need to mother me, boss. I'm doing fine. Besides, Chef Jana's all in my face about that kind of stuff anyways."

Witt laughed. For all his teenage bravado,

Jose had a lot of insight and could read people exceptionally well. "Jana mothers you?"

"She's always asking me when I last called my mom, how I'm getting along with Mateo, whether or not I've got a girlfriend—you know, the kind of stuff women care about." Jose said it with a ridiculous, jaded tolerance that belonged on a thirty-five-year-old, not someone just out of high school. "She wants me to think about cooking school."

Witt had come to the same conclusion, actually. "She's right—about the school, that is. And calling your mom." He didn't care to get into the details of Jose's dating life—he'd leave that to Jana's interpersonal curiosity. "You should look into it." He swallowed a sense of guilt about the last time he'd called his own mother—it had been entirely too long.

Jose patted the truck. "My school's right here, dude." The kid treated the truck like… well, like a girlfriend. Like a teenager treats his first car. Perhaps, for a kid like Jose, the truck was his first proud possession of sorts. Jose took his job of keeping the truck clean very seriously. More than once Witt had looked up to see Jose pull a blue bandanna from his pocket and polish a fender or bumper. "Chef's teaching me all kinds of stuff. I never thought I'd say this, but I like it. I like cooking. I'd never get a chance to do something like this back in Martins Gap, you know? Back there, I'd probably be stuck washing dishes at Lolly's diner or ringing up pizzas at Shorty's."

Witt felt a surge of satisfaction. Here, in front of him, was Gunner's dream—a dream Witt had been happily grafted into—of what the Blue Thorn could be for Martins Gap. The town was a nice place, but opportunities were limited. Gunner and Ellie's store had already brought people into town, had given back to the community, and now they were reaching beyond its borders. Whether he realized it or not, Gunner Buckton Jr. was becoming the community pillar his grandfather had once been, the man of integrity people had once discounted him ever being. Witt's role in that leadership fueled something deep, something Witt knew he would never have quite grasped if he'd stayed at Star Beef. His father's business was strong and prosperous—but it was set in its ways. There was nothing for Witt to build there, nothing for him to grow. Looking at Jose, talking to a scruffy kid he'd once seen only as counter help about considering a culinary career, Witt knew he'd made the right choice.

"Jana can teach you a lot, it's true. But there's even more to learn. Pretty soon you'll be ready to learn more than this truck can teach you." He turned to look the boy straight in the eye. "When that time comes, I want to help you look at culinary schools. The applications, all that stuff? I'll help. I won't like losing you, but I'll gladly lose you to the next step in your career."

Jose ran a hand through his wild mane. "You mean like college?"

The astonishment in the kid's voice dug into Witt's heart. "Like whatever you want. College for business, cooking school, wherever you want to go. You're sharp, Jose. You could do a lot of things beyond flirting with all the *Azulo* girls." Witt had resisted Jose's name for the Blue Thorn truck customers—born from the Spanish *azul*, the word for blue—but the term had taken on a life of its own.

"I love the *Azulos*," Jose said with a heart-slayer grin. "Best part of my job."

"I'll admit—" Witt laughed "—customer relations is your personal specialty. But I'm serious. I think you can go places, and I want you to know we're eager to help you get there. After we get through this first season, that is. Right now, you're indispensable to operations."

Jose pulled a baseball cap from his back pocket and put it on. "Indispensable. I like the sound of that."

"Just as long as indispensable doesn't turn into cocky and showing up late." Witt bumped his shoulder against Jose's. "Don't let anything I said go to your head."

"Oh, no worries there. Chef can be harsh, man. That woman's got a temper." Again, the kid had a strange knack for sounding decades older than he was.

"Don't I know it." Witt felt strange commiserating about Jana with a teenager. Still, they'd both been the target of Jana's fierce opinions and her fearless way of sharing them.

"Thing is, she fights because she cares. You see that, boss, don't you?" For a moment the sincerity of the sentiment looked out of place on his young features, until Jose rolled his eyes in an entirely too teenage fashion. "It's not so bad, until she's all up in your face about the lettuce."

In fact, Jana was out talking to a new produce vendor because she'd pitched a bit of a fit over the quality—or lack thereof—of last week's lettuce and tomatoes. Witt gave a low, commiserating laugh. "That was something, wasn't it?"

"One thing's for sure. I don't ever want to

be the guy who wrongs that woman. *Ella es un tornado, sí?*"

The question required no translation. Jana was, in many ways, a storm—powerful, dangerous, but a little bit thrilling at the same time.

That was Jose—always seeing just a little bit too much.

"So you question his motives for wanting to enter the food truck rodeo?" Ellie made the inquiry to Jana while looking longingly into a yarn-shop window they passed. Ellie was downtown Saturday morning making some wedding arrangements, and they were walking to breakfast before Jana started her day on the truck.

Jana smiled at the woman's continual obsession—Ellie must have all the yarn she could ever want from her own bison fiber business, and she still couldn't help looking at more to buy. "I'm not sure what to think," she admitted. "Did you know about the food truck rodeo contest?"

Ellie dragged her gaze away from the display window. "Of course I did. The Austin Restaurateurs Association is one of the sponsors."

"So why didn't you mention it to Witt?"

"I didn't think y'all were ready. I didn't want to make Witt feel like we were pressuring him to enter. And we're not. He's so far ahead of schedule that I'd probably talk him out of it if I could—no one needs things to be going as fast as they are. Sure, it would be a coup to win that prize money but not if you don't think you're ready to enter. Trouble is, it may be hard to talk him out of it now—since Cole brought it up."

Jana recalled Witt's icy glare when he'd caught sight of his brother-in-law. "Those two are really frosty toward each other, aren't they?"

"It was a hard blow when Uncle Grayson brought Cole on at Star Beef. Buckton men are a stubborn lot, that's for sure. Gunner would have probably left the country in a furious huff if our dad had ever pulled a move like that. They wouldn't be on speaking terms, that's for certain. Actually, Gunner and Dad *weren't* speaking when Dad passed." Ellie sighed. "But that's another story."

Jana pulled open the coffee house door. "I'm not sure I'd call whatever communication took place between Cole, Mary and Witt 'speaking.' More like verbal sparring, or something male bison do to each other."

Ellie laughed. "Charge, you mean? Lock horns and bellow?"

The image fit. "That sounds about right," Jana replied. "I just can't help thinking Witt's urge to do this is more about proving something to Cole than it is about moving Blue Thorn Burgers forward."

"It's both," Ellie offered as she slipped into a booth by a sunny window framed in rustic burlap-and-lace curtains. "Witt's a lot of things, but foolish isn't one of them. His motives may be mixed, I'll admit, but it seems to me that both motives would be all the more reason for him to be certain you can make a good showing before entering. The last thing Witt wants to do is give Cole any more cause to look down on him, which would happen if the truck made a poor showing in the contest." Ellie gave Jana a long look. "Witt believes in you. He wouldn't suggest this if he didn't think y'all would come out on top, or close to it. I don't know if you've noticed, but my cousin doesn't do things he can't do well." She sighed. "I think it's one of the reasons he came to Blue Thorn, actually. He doesn't play second fiddle to anyone easily."

"But he works for you and Gunner."

Ellie waved the statement away. "Oh, he doesn't work for me. It may be the family ranch, but no one is under any illusions that it isn't really Gunner in charge. I think even Gran's conceded that point by now."

"My point exactly," Jana said as she nodded to the server, who stood by the table with a pot of coffee. Jana hadn't slept well since Wednesday, tossing and turning over the food truck rodeo suggestion. She was uncomfortable for more reasons than just Witt's motives. The prospect of all that contest publicity made her nervous. She'd decided to let go of such fears, hadn't she? *Reggie can't keep me from living my life.* Squaring her shoulders, Jana returned her focus to the here and now. "He's fine working for Gunner but not for Cole?"

Ellie pointed toward her own cup, inhaling as the potent aroma wafted up from the filled mug and smiling her thanks at the server. "Gunner gives Witt a free hand with the meat business—he knows the ranching better than anyone, but he'd be the first one to admit Witt has a better handle on the retail stuff." Ellie leaned in. "I don't think Cole would be so generous, if that's what you're asking."

Jana had to ask. "So you don't think Cole is goading him into this?"

"Oh, I expect Cole *is* goading him into this. I know Mary loves Cole to pieces, and they're a good couple, but that man has a competitive streak a mile wide. Not that he's being mean. Cole probably thinks he's providing Witt with incentive. A chance to prove himself and all." She shook her head. "Cole isn't a Buckton by birth, but he sure is one by temperament."

"And your fiancé?" Jana had to wonder if anything less than an iron-willed man would dare marry into the Buckton family. But surely Nash was up to the challenge. The man was taking over as Martins Gap's sheriff in a matter of days, after all.

The glow that came over that woman's face was downright adorable. "Oh, Nash can hold his own. Not quite as stubborn, in my opinion, but just as strong."

"Not that you're biased or anything." Jana watched Ellie's fingers stray to the beautiful diamond on her left hand. It was nice to see Ellie so happy. Her previous engagement had been a messy public disaster, finding her chef fiancé in the arms of the woman who would have been her maid of honor. The whole restaurant chain had talked of nothing else for weeks.

"Oh, I'm totally biased," Ellie said with a wide grin. "And totally happy. And totally busy. We've rolled out our fourth product line and the wedding is in six weeks." Her eyes went wide. "You got your invitation, didn't you? You're coming? You've got to come—you're like part of the family now."

Jana appreciated how fully welcomed into the Buckton clan she felt. This large, loud family was strange but intriguing—certainly not something she was used to. When Mom came for Thanksgiving it would be just the two of them and a tiny roasted turkey breast. Somehow, with the Bucktons, the clash and chaos just added to the appeal. "I wouldn't miss it."

"It'll be close after the rodeo, now that I think of it," Ellie said after she ordered her huevos rancheros. "You and Witt will need a party after all that. I did put a plus-one on your invite. Have you thought about who you want to bring?"

Jana ordered her eggs sunny-side up, ignoring her curiosity as to who Witt's plus-one would be. Witt's social life wasn't her concern. He never talked about being in a relationship. There were times, however—moments where he was tired or unguarded—where she felt a tug between them that extended beyond professional. They surely couldn't go together. A family dinner at the Blue Thorn was one thing, but a wedding? That was a whole other level of social interaction—one she wasn't quite sure she was ready for. Besides, Jana had a feeling things might be tense enough between them after this whole food truck rodeo business.

Then again, if Witt was right and things went really well for them in the contest, the situation might be…well, really good between them. And what would that mean?

"Wedding dates are just a whole other level of torture when you're not in a relationship, you know?" Jana spooned sugar into her coffee. "I have no idea if I'll take anyone at all. I barely have time to get my laundry done these days, much less find a well-dressed man ready to take on the likes of your family."

Ellie smirked. "You don't have carnivorous males lining up outside the truck? Witt makes jokes, but honestly, the way you look and the way you cook? It's not hard to believe it could happen."

Jana rolled her eyes. "Please, not you, too."

"No, not me. I'm not on the 'burger truck as man magnet' bandwagon—or girl magnet for that matter, from what I've heard about Jose's antics—so don't you worry about that. Happy customers? Yes. Datable men? I'm not so sure." The server set down their orders and Ellie dug in as she continued talking. "What about your church? Witt says you like

Awakenings. Or if you've been looking for a change, you were such a hit at the picnic, you know you're welcome at MGCC anytime you want. I'll tell you, though, the single-male population out by us is mighty slim pickings. You don't strike me as going for the cowboy type."

Jana shook her head. "I'm not looking. The truck is where my focus needs to be. I've got no energy for relationships now. Soon, maybe, but not now."

"And if God's got other ideas?" Ellie bore those dreamy googly eyes Jana associated with all women engaged or recently married. A "the whole world should be as happy as I am" glow that was at once endearing and annoying.

"Then He's going to need to make me an eighth day of the week. And if we get anywhere in this rodeo business, maybe even a ninth day." She looked at Ellie. "Do y'all really want a fleet of trucks and two restaurants? Do you want this part of the business to be that big?" She knew how Witt would answer that question, but she wanted to hear what Ellie thought.

"Witt does dream big, doesn't he?" She set down her fork. "I think we could have more than one truck, and maybe a place to eat out by the ranch. But honestly, those are Witt's dreams. I want the ranch to stick around another three generations. I want the bison yarn to do well, so that I can contribute to the ranch's success in my own way. The rest of the master plan? I pretty much leave that to Witt and Gunner."

"And what about Gunner? What does he think of Witt's grand plan?"

"I think he's willing to let Witt run with the ball—or is that the burger?" she quipped with a giggle "—as far as he can. Ranches are a tough business. Every income stream we can add to the mix keeps us healthy and able to weather a rough patch. I don't think Gunner dreams of a sprawling empire, though. Just a strong, healthy business that can support our families for the next generations."

It sounded like so much more than a business venture when Ellie put it like that. It sounded like Blue Thorn Ranch was a piece of history, an essential part of the family's identity. And now she was part of that. This was so much bigger than her and the puny dislike of publicity Ronnie Taylor had given her.

"The rodeo could be really good for all of Blue Thorn," Jana said, thinking out loud. She could barely believe she was coming around to the idea. "It would draw a lot of attention to the ranch, and to all that you're doing out there."

"Could be good for you, as well," Ellie agreed. "I think you'll grill their socks off."

Who knows? Jana thought as she started in on her eggs. *Maybe I will.*

Chapter Eleven

She'd relented. Within days, Jana had given her consent to entering the contest. Now, on the first weekend in December, Jana found herself a contestant in the Austin Holiday Food Truck Rodeo's first round.

Rodeo really was the right word. The park was a crazy, chaotic circus of thirty food trucks selling everything from cupcakes to Cuban sandwiches. Most food truck rodeos were simply rolling food fests, social collections during which a variety of vendors gathered to make a fun event where people could try a wide selection of different foods.

This one had the added element of a competition, with two levels of ballots—one cast by food critics, the other cast by customers. Customers roamed the circle of trucks, sampling what they wished, and then casting ballots by either texting the truck number—a large black "16" was currently fixed above the Blue Thorn Burgers counter window—or filling out a paper ballot at a big red holiday sleigh in the center of the circle. There were semifinals and finals to come if they made it that far.

"I can't decide if it's more of a food competition or a popularity contest," she remarked to Witt as they worked together to serve the long line of customers. Where that man had found a turquoise Santa-style ski hat to wear—or how he'd found the nerve to wear it—she might never know. She was only glad he hadn't asked her or Jose to don one of the silly things.

"One place where a long line is okay?" he said, flipping the ridiculous yellow pom-pon out of his way as he pulled more buns from the cabinet behind them.

"Yeah, I'll give you this one." Competition wasn't usually her thing, but as she cast a quick glance around the circle and saw that the Blue Thorn had one of the longest lines of the bunch, Jana felt her determination grow. They actually had a shot at this. She knew her food was great, and placing high in this could let the rest of the world know. Out of the corner of her eye she watched one man roll his eyes back with gastronomic pleasure as he took a bite of his burger. He handed the food to his friend and immediately took out his phone, texting his vote. Or a friend. Or, she hoped, both.

"Hey there, stranger!"

Jana's eyes snapped back to the customer window to see an old friend from culinary school waving hello. "Marion!" she called. "What are you doing in Austin?"

Marion beamed. "Got a job at the Driskill, darlin'."

Marion had every reason to beam. The Driskill ranked as one of the swankiest hotels in Austin. A position there would be a feather in any chef's hat. It wasn't surprising; Marion had been a star pastry chef in school. Jana had had the extra pounds at graduation to prove it. If she'd been after such a post, Marion would have just given Jana reason to be jealous. Only Jana wasn't interested in that kind of career. She really liked where she was, and felt genuine excitement over where she was going. "Good for you," she offered with true happiness as she slid the next order to its waiting customer and put three more burgers on the grill.

"I saw you on the news the other morning—I had no idea you were in Austin, either." Marion fished a business card from her jeans pocket and placed it on the counter. "Gimme a call—we can catch up when you're not cleaning up your competition here. My boyfriend just ate one of your burgers and he sure voted for you."

Jana grabbed the card and tucked it in her pocket. "Thanks, I'll do that."

"You go, girl! Grill your way to victory!" Marion gave a big thumbs-up and headed back to a tall young man in a cowboy hat who was finishing up the last of his burger. Jana wasn't surprised Marion had ended up in Texas—a quintessential Georgia peach, Marion had always had a thing for the cowboy type.

The rest of the rodeo became a nonstop stream of orders, pressures and, thankfully, praises. There were two other burger trucks in the circle, but neither of them boasted the lines the Blue Thorn truck enjoyed. Maybe Witt's theory on long lines wasn't so wrong after all. Jana could calculate that the Blue Thorn Burgers truck was a favorite among the burger crowd, but even that didn't mean success—the rodeo didn't differentiate between categories. That meant a cupcake truck could edge out a burger truck for any spot in the ranking—an extra layer of pressure, to be sure.

It was nearly 11:00 p.m., just as Jana and Jose were giving the counters a final wipe-down, when Witt hopped in the truck, the silly hat gone but a huge grin on his face.

"We came in third!" he declared, holding up a scoring sheet.

"We make it to the next round," Jose crowed, breaking into a little dance and flicking his dishrag around for extra flair. "Blue Thorn has got it goin' on," he half sang, ending with a flourish of what Jana hoped were compliments and boasts in Spanish.

Jana sat down on the stool, the work of the night finally pulling aches from her back and neck now that her adrenaline rush had faded. "Third, huh? Well, what do you know? Who took first?"

"Frostings," Witt replied.

"The cupcakes. Of course. Why am I not surprised?"

"I don't get the whole cupcake thing," Jose mused. "Too small. Too much frosting. I'd take a doughnut over a cupcake any day. There's a maple bacon one from a shop down on South Congress that beats any cupcake I've ever eaten."

"I've had it," Witt agreed. "So good."

"I know, right?" Jose sent the dish towel, with a perfect basketball swish, into the dirty-linens container. "You wouldn't think it works but man, it does."

"And second place?" Jana asked.

"It's gonna get you fired up," Witt warned. "I'm not sure I should tell you."

"I can handle it," Jana said as she gave him a look. "Who is it?"

"Toast."

Witt was right—it did fire her up. "The sandwich truck?"

Witt pointed at her. "The grilled cheese people. I went over there and they were pushing their grilled cheese tonight."

Jana stood up off the stool. "You ate at Toast tonight?" She probably shouldn't have given it the air of accusation she did, but she was tired.

"I checked out our competition, that's all." Witt put his hands up. "I had a friend buy it—nobody saw me standing in line—their *long* line—to buy Toast's grilled cheese."

Jana crossed her hands over her chest, surprisingly indignant at the thought of Witt eating anyone else's grilled cheese. "And?"

"Relax, Chef. Yours is better."

Jana unclenched her fists, relieved. This whole competition thing was bringing out a side of her she didn't recognize and didn't especially like.

"But theirs has photos," Witt added, and was rewarded with a well-targeted wet dish-rag *thwack*-ing against his stomach.

"Third!" Witt proclaimed as he peeled the dishrag from his shirt and tossed it in the hamper. "I would have been happy just to make the top ten, but third!" His gave Jose an affectionate cuff on the shoulder, then held her gaze for a long moment. "I think we really can take this thing. I truly think we have a shot."

For the first time since Witt had raised this crazy idea, Jana did, too. "We might," she offered carefully. She would have ranked taking first place after such a short time in business a near impossibility last night. Tonight, the happy customers, the high vote count and the glow in Witt's eyes made the impossible seem a little more possible.

"Third," he said again, scanning the sheet as if the rankings might cheat and change behind his back. "It's amazing."

"I'd go out and celebrate if I weren't dead on my feet," Jana said.

"Exhausting night, huh?" Witt looked a bit disappointed, as if he could stay up all night celebrating. Of course, he hadn't been scrambling behind the counter for the past six hours—he had extra energy to revel in their victory.

She could go out. Part of her felt too wound up from the night's efforts to go straight home. The wiser part of her, however, knew she was too tired. Why? Because she wanted to hug Witt in congratulations. People made dumb choices when they were tired. People blurred professional lines when they were tired and celebrating. No, the smartest thing would be to take the truck home and go to bed. "I'm spent," she said, slipping her knife kit into her messenger bag along with the soiled blue chef's coat. She watched Witt smile as he noticed that she'd tied one of the Blue Thorn bandannas around the strap of the messenger bag. "I'm grimy, besides." Even the dim reflection in the truck's windshield told her she was pretty much a sweaty mess and nothing that should be out in a restaurant or coffee shop before a long, hot shower.

"Okay then. We'll find another way to celebrate tomorrow." Witt took the score sheet and fixed it to one of the back cabinets with a magnet. "Great work, everybody." He gave Jose a fist bump, managed an awkward "I'm not sure if I should touch you" wave to Jana and stepped down out of the truck.

"I think I'm going for doughnuts," Jose declared, slipping his backpack over his shoulder. "Some friends came in from Martins Gap to root for us, and we haven't had a chance to all hang out together in a while. It's early for someone my age."

Jana laughed. "You do that. Have one of those maple bacon things for me."

"I'll bring you one tomorrow morning," he replied as he pushed open the back door and headed toward his bike. "They're totally awesome."

Jana shook her head as she found her keys and put them in the truck's ignition. It really had been a good night, and she really was dead on her feet.

She made it all the way to the apartment parking lot, parked the truck and was in the elevator heading up to her floor before the thing niggling at the back of her mind all night hit her:

Marion had been friends with Ronnie. And Marion now knew where she was.

Chapter Twelve

❧

They were in the semifinals. They could actually win.

For a while, Witt had thought it was just his competitive streak firing up, the long-burning desire to show up Cole and Mary distorting his assessment of Blue Thorn Burgers's capabilities. But as he lent a hand in the truck the following Tuesday, scrambling beside Jose and Jana as they served the ever-growing lines of hungry customers, he began to truly believe they had a shot. That buzz, that indefinable thing that took good restaurants and made them go-to spots, that vibe everybody wanted but no one knew exactly how to create, was coming to them.

He caught Jana's eye as yet another new fan's eyes popped with delight on their first bite. After the first round of the rodeo, Jose had launched an "#Azulos" hashtag on social media that was actually taking off. "Do you see that?" he called to her, pointing to the young man now enthusiastically chomping on his burger.

"I sure do," she called back, her eyes bright and radiant. Watching Jana cook—when it seemed like the whole world funneled down to that woman and her food—was enthralling. You could light the whole truck from the energy vibrating off her. If sparks weren't flying out of her fingertips, they ought to be. She was so alive when she cooked. She was something he wanted to be next to, to draw vibrancy from, to touch. More than once he fought back the urge to grab one of those hands and see if he could really feel the electricity he was sure was there.

It was a good thing they were crazy busy, because that's the only thing that overpowered the growing urge. Her singular, powerful sense of purpose when she cooked called to some deep and unmoored part of him. When he'd left Star Beef, he hadn't quite known where he belonged. He knew, now, with a growing solidness of surety, that *here* was where he belonged. He wasn't just the extended-family add-on. He was the force behind Blue Thorn Burgers—however big that turned out to be.

And it was looking like it would turn out to be very big. To take this contest after only a few months in operation? He couldn't begin to estimate the splash that would generate in the Austin restaurant scene.

"Chef, no, he wanted slaw," Jose said as he slid an order back to Jana.

Getting an order wrong? That wasn't like Jana at all.

"Yeah, right. Sure. Upsize their drink to make up for the wait while I fix it, okay?" Jana spun around to get the slaw, knocking over a container of sauce in the process. An uncharacteristic cry of frustration came from her—normally she was elegantly quiet when she cooked—so he ducked over to tend to the mess for her. It brought them shoulder to shoulder, and Witt noticed the vibe he thought he'd seen a minute ago wasn't quite right.

"You okay?" he asked as he mopped up the sauce and retrieved another container from the fridge.

"Fine," she said with too much of an edge to be true.

"You can slow down, you know," he offered. "I'm a big fan of long lines, remember?"

"And I'm not." She wiped her brow with a

blue bandanna. She didn't have makeup on. Not that he cared—she was beautiful without it—but it was just another detail that seemed off this morning.

As he darted back to his post at the register, Witt gave Jose a "what's up?" look.

Jose's silent reply of a narrowed eye and a shrug effectively said, *Something's up, but I don't know what it is.*

Witt looked at Jana again as he rung up another customer. She did look more drained than usual. "You sure you're all right?" he asked again.

This time she looked at him. "A little tired."

It may have been a mistake to extend the operating hours in the days between the rodeo's first round and the semifinals tomorrow night, even if it was Jana's idea. She might be spreading herself too thin.

"Maybe it would be good to shut down at three. Just for an hour or so to give everyone a break. We've been at it since ten and we're scheduled to go all the way until eleven tonight."

He watched those words dull whatever sparks were left in her eyes. This wasn't just fatigue. He leaned close to whisper in her ear—something he'd never done and a move that made him wildly aware of how close they were. "We can say we need to run for supplies or something."

She stilled for just a moment, and he could practically feel her exhale. "Maybe."

"Maybe nothing. It's 2:15. I'm going out there to cut the line off. At this rate we'll need more supplies soon anyway. I'd much rather run out in the middle of the afternoon than smack dab in the middle of the dinner rush."

He had a strange moment of awareness as he went out and told the person currently in the back of the line that they would be the last served. This was an odd new Witt—turning away sales. Somehow the choke hold Dad, Mary and Cole had on his self-worth—a grip he knew was more his doing than the result of some ill will on their part—was loosening. The success the Blue Thorn truck was seeing made it easier not to need the success so much. There were other things that were more important.

After a short chat with the people in line, Witt looked back at Jana working frantically in the truck. His earlier hunch had been correct—something wasn't right. Normally she kept a laser-tight focus on the food and the next customer. In fact, he knew Jana's ability to make a rich, split-second connection with customers as she handed them their food was crucial to their success. People loved her as much as they loved her food.

Today, however, her eyes darted over the heads of the customers, scanning the area around the truck. Looking for something. Someone? She wasn't expecting a guest or friend to come by—her face had too tight an expression, more apprehension than expectation.

"Heard this place is great," someone said behind him. "Think the line is worth it?"

"Definitely," Witt said as he turned to face a middle-aged couple who had mistaken him for standing in line. "But I'm out here to let you know we've sold out for now." Witt extended a hand, and pointed to the Blue Thorn Burgers logo on his blue shirt. "We'll go restock and be back by 4:30." He reached into his pocket for the one-dollar-off business card coupons he kept handy for luring new customers to the truck. "Take this and we'll see you when we get back."

"Sold out, huh?" the woman said, a little disappointed but not nearly as much as Witt feared. "Well, I guess that means your burgers are as good as everyone says."

"Come back to the rodeo tomorrow night, and I guarantee you they'll be *better* than everyone says. And then you can vote for us in the semifinals."

"Well, aren't you an enterprising young man," she said. "I predict you'll go far."

"I sure hope so." Witt turned to look at Jana, convinced his decision to give her a break was the right one. *Thanks for that bit of wisdom, Lord. Keep us all safe and healthy while we're on this crazy ride, okay?*

Jana's shoulders felt like two giant piles of knots. Witt had indeed forced them to take the break he'd promised. Before anyone could object, he'd taken the wheel and driven the truck up to the top of a parking garage, sending Jose down the street for coffees. She and Witt sat in the back doorway, taking in the breeze and the surprisingly lovely view.

"I never knew this spot was even here," she said, feeling the height and the sky take her stress down a notch with every breath. There was even a set of cheery flower boxes blooming in the corner—a secret little oasis in the middle of the busy city.

"Mark told me about this place. His band comes here after gigs." Witt leaned back on his hands, the breeze blowing his hair across his forehead. "The height tends to lend a bit of perspective, you know?"

"It does." Jana discovered she was even more tense than she'd realized. *Just because you're getting noticed doesn't mean Ronnie is watching. You're just letting your fatigue play tricks on your mind. That jerk is long gone and years in your past. Keep him there.*

She turned to see Witt staring at her. "*Are* you okay?" The concern in his eyes made her both nervous and grateful. She knew it wasn't smart for him to care about her—but she was glad he did, all the same.

"I'm fine." She said it quickly and loudly enough that both of them knew that was a lie. "I'm just nervous," she admitted. "I hadn't realized how much I want to win this thing." It was true—Witt had ignited a new determination in her, as if his pie-in-the-sky thinking was rubbing off—but it wasn't the whole truth.

"Don't work yourself too hard. We've still got two rounds to go yet."

She pulled back, mock concern in her eyes. "Who are you and what have you done with my Witt Buckton?" She immediately regretted the "my"—and the fact that he'd noticed it, as well.

His smile was warm if a bit cautious. "I admit, this moderation thing is new territory for me. But you looked…I don't know…off today. Like something was bothering you or you were waiting for some other shoe to drop. I need to keep an eye out for the health and safety of my secret weapon, you know."

She laughed. It was just like Witt to view her as an asset. But his expression said there was more to it than that. Did the emotional tug she always felt around him go both ways? If so, what was she going to do about it? *I'm too tired and rattled to handle this right now, Lord. Don't let me allow things to venture where they shouldn't go. Not when we're on the brink of something wonderful.*

"Relax," she assured. "Your secret weapon just needs a better night's sleep. But," she continued, rolling her shoulders, "I agree. I needed this break."

"So you're sure you're okay?"

The way he pressed made her actually consider telling Witt everything. *And then you'll look like a skittish little girl, someone with no confidence and no future. Don't you dare let Ronnie win like that. He's a shadow. A bad memory, better forgotten. This man is your boss, not your confessor.*

"I'm not afraid of hard work, boss."

"I know that. Here, turn around."

"What?"

Witt spun his finger. "Turn your back to me."

She felt her spine tighten. "Why?"

"Consider it a management request."

She rolled her eyes, but shifted herself around until her back was to Witt. He placed her hands on her shoulders, and then pure bliss descended on her as his strong hands began to knead the knots in her shoulders. "Where'd you learn to do that?" she managed to gasp out in her near-melty state.

"College. Crew rowers get really sore shoulders. Massage techniques are useful to know if you're on the men's team, but *dating gold* if you're anywhere near the women's team. I owe my social life to these hands— what skimpy social life I had in college, that is."

Jana let her head fall to one side. "Skimpy? You probably had lines longer than the truck's."

He let out a low laugh. "Now you know where my love of long lines came from."

His voice was warm—the kind of tone where she could hear the way his smile colored the words. She was acutely aware of his presence behind her, and just as acutely grateful they weren't face-to-face. All the things that were so appealing about Witt Buckton were piling up around her, and she was too tired and nerve-racked to fight them off.

She should tell him about Ronnie. He

clearly cared about her safety, about her well-being, and right now Ronnie was managing to become a threat to both. Maybe the whole business wouldn't freak her out so much if someone else knew. Witt would probably tell her what a ludicrous idea it was to think that Ronnie would bridge so many years and hundreds of miles to track her down just because of a couple of press interviews. He was probably unhappily married with three kids and a nervous wife by now, and never even gave her a moment's thought.

Witt's massage became more vigorous. "You need extra energy. We're gonna have to sturdy you up if the truck keeps on like this. Personal trainer? Nutrition specialist?"

The teasing in his words broke the moment, and she twisted around to eye him. "You'd sic a nutrition specialist on a chef? That'd be like me sending you a math tutor."

He winced comically. "Ouch. I guess I see your point."

"And I don't need anyone standing over me telling me to do more sit-ups." Most of her knew he was teasing, but the small part of her that hated anyone implying she was weak or vulnerable roared up in defense the way it always did. Ronnie's legacy was her bone-deep need to feel strong. To be seen as strong.

Jana Powers was never going to be anyone to mess with ever again. "I'm fine," she said with extra emphasis. "I'm ready for this."

Witt held up his hands. "Okay, okay, I didn't mean anything by it."

She gave him her best glower. "Then why'd you say it? Why did you imply I needed bolstering up?"

"I didn't mean it like that. I…I think I was just trying to show that I realize what a demanding job this is. I…"

"Don't you two kids make me come back there!" Jose called from the front of the truck. She hadn't even heard him come in. "Ay," he said, in a spot-on *mama* impersonation, "I turn my back for five minutes and you two are bickering like dogs."

Witt shot Jana a "can you believe him" look before standing up to yank his coffee cup from the cardboard carrier Jose held. "How old are you again?"

"I'll be twenty in six months."

"You sound like you'll be forty in six days," Jana countered as she accepted the coffee from Jose. It was burn-your-fingers hot and smelled blissfully strong—just the way she liked it. And large enough that by the time she got to the bottom of it, she'd be recharged and ready for the dinner rush.

Because she was strong. And she was ready. Tonight and at tomorrow's semifinals, the world was going to see just how good Jana Powers could grill.

Chapter Thirteen

Witt watched Jana smile victoriously for the camera Thursday morning. She was being interviewed about their spectacular showing last night, placing them in Saturday night's final round. "I'm thrilled to move on to the finals. I can't wait to show Austin how fabulous Blue Thorn burgers taste. If you've never had a bison burger, you're about to learn just how delicious a good, basic burger can be."

The reporter held up a burger to the camera, then took a bite. "Believe that woman," he said with his mouth still full. "And get down here for the final round of the Austin Holiday Food Truck Rodeo. Reporting live from the Blue Thorn Burgers truck, this is Dave Carson. Back to you, Tony."

The bright camera lights switched off, and Dave took another healthy bite as Witt walked up to his celebrity chef. He was glad he'd de-clined to do any part of the interview, instead giving the morning's full spotlight to Jana. She'd charmed the socks off that reporter.

"I owe you an apology, Jana," Dave said as he put the microphone down.

"Why?" Jana replied. "That was a great in-terview. You've probably given us a terrific head start on the finals."

"It's not about this interview," Dave admit-ted. He licked a bit of Jana's signature sauce off his finger. "It's about my other life." Dave motioned for them to walk away from the crowd of people who had gathered for the taping.

"Your other life?"

"I'm Spatula Dave."

Witt nearly dropped the coffee he was holding. "You're Spatula Dave?"

"Shh," Dave said, looking around. "For ob-vious reasons, I can't really let that get out."

Jana's defenses had already gone up. "You're Spatula Dave?" Her tone was not as-tonishment. It was annoyance. Witt gulped and began to wonder if Jana was about to undo all the good that interview had just done.

"Play nice..." he warned her, only half jok-ing. "He *did* say he owed you an apology."

"He sure does," Jana replied.

"I came down hard on you when you first opened," Dave admitted. "You deserved it then."

"Did we, now?" Jana cut in, her fingers flexing and straightening. Witt readied himself to grab her arm if she started winding up for a punch. As Jose had said, the woman was a *tornado*, and Spatula Dave had really gotten under her skin. Witt readied every diplomatic skill he possessed and shot up an instantaneous prayer for grace and peace.

"You *don't* deserve it now," Dave went on. "And I'm big enough to admit it. You're really good, and people should know it. So tomorrow you're going to read Spatula Dave's first-ever recant. I'm going to give you a great review, and set it to post tomorrow, before Saturday's finals."

Spatula Dave was going to issue his first-ever recant and praise Blue Thorn Burgers? The day before the Rodeo finals? Witt couldn't buy that kind of publicity with all the money in Texas. "That's great," Witt offered. He looked at Jana, who seemed pleased but puzzled. "It's fabulous news, isn't it, Chef Jana?"

"I am glad to hear it," Jana said. "But I am curious as to what changed your mind. Sure, we've made some changes since we first opened, but nothing big enough to require a recant. If you didn't like us then, why do you like us now?"

Dave shrugged. "I don't think it was any one thing. I admit, some of this is my fault. I try to make a policy of visiting a place four times before I post a review. I didn't in your case, and I need to put that right."

"I sure appreciate it." Witt smiled broadly at Dave, but noticed Jana wasn't smiling yet. "We both do."

"Why didn't you give us a fair shot?" Jana asked. Witt considered taking her by the arm and hauling her back into the truck before she dismantled all of Spatula Dave's goodwill. This wasn't the time for her stubbornness. This fell squarely in the lemons-to-lemonade column—this new praise would get more coverage now than Dave's first ding ever did—but Jana obviously didn't see it that way.

Dave paused, and Witt sent up a second burst of prayer for calm.

"My mother died," the reporter offered softly.

Dave's admission sucked all the air out of Jana's resentment. Her expression changed completely. "I'm sorry." Witt could see that she truly meant it.

"I was under a ton of pressure at work at

the time and I was short on content. I cut corners. I hope my next post and the bit we just taped make up for it. That's why I told you who I am. But I'm going to have to swear you to secrecy, okay? Spatula Dave will be over and done if people know who I am and can see me coming."

"We completely understand," Witt offered, almost dizzy with relief, and regretting the comment he'd made way back about Spatula Dave having bison burger baggage. It felt insensitive and mean knowing what he knew now. Spatula Dave was a human being, not an internet troll. "I'm sorry for your loss. I'm sure it's a terrible blow to lose a parent."

The fresh grief in Dave's eyes reminded Witt that it hadn't been that long since that first review—since the woman's death—even if it felt like the truck had traveled a million miles since then. "Yeah," was all Dave replied, choking a bit on even that one word.

To Witt's surprise, Jana reached out and touched Dave's elbow. "Thank you for changing your mind. It means a lot to all of us that you'd issue a recant."

"Journalistic objectivity aside," Dave confided, "I hope you win. I'm sick of the cupcakes and the tacos getting all the glory in this town." They all laughed at that—the other two trucks in the final featured those foods. Jana had been uncharacteristically gleeful about Toast's grilled cheese not making the finals, but he'd give her that victory for the moment. "I'll be back Saturday night to cover the winning truck, so here's hoping we talk again soon."

"If we do, your burger's on the house," Witt added, then handed Dave a stack of the business card discount coupons. "Bring a few friends."

Dave waved as he headed back to the television truck. "Count on it."

Witt looked at Jana once Dave had left. "I didn't see that coming."

Jana put one hand to her forehead. "I didn't, either. I spent so much time being annoyed at my vision of a mean, nasty Spatula Dave that I can't quite square that with the guy I just met." She looked up at Witt. "Lesson learned, huh?"

They started walking back toward the truck. "I thought you were gonna slug him there for a minute. It's never safe to insult your cooking, is it?"

She shrugged. "I admit, I can get a bit defensive."

"A bit? Like the Gulf of Mexico is a bit of a pond?"

"Okay, okay, I get it."

He put his hand on her elbow to stop her. "But hey, that interview you gave him? Great stuff. I don't think you realize your talent for media. It's a gift—you can't learn that stuff. It's just in you or it isn't. And it's definitely in you."

She narrowed her eyes, but playfully this time—not the version she'd given Dave before his heart-wrenching admission. "Don't you go all adventure burger spokesmodel on me." The term had become her not-entirely-joking way of letting him know when he was on the verge of focusing too much attention her way. He knew this rodeo was pushing her to her limit on that front.

"Two more days, then you can revel in your obscurity clear through New Year's."

She laughed. "Like that's going to happen with you around."

As he climbed into the truck, Witt fought the urge to sit her down and massage her shoulders again. He was embarrassed how wonderful it felt to touch her—it was getting harder to discount the illogical attraction he felt toward someone who pushed so many of his buttons. "Thank you," he said.

"For what? For not slugging Spatula Dave?"

He settled on holding her gaze a second

longer than was necessary, still captured by how her eyes could be so bright and so dark at the same time. "For being so good at what you do."

Witt was pleased to see the compliment catch her off guard. "I suppose I could say the same about you."

For someone with all her confidence and drive, she always seemed so startled when he offered praise. It made him want to compliment her every chance he got—a rather dangerous urge for someone who was supposed to be her boss. "We make a good team."

"We do," she admitted with a warm smile.

"Hello! Has everyone forgotten the other member of this awesome team?" Jose called from his post, up to his elbows in suds at the sink.

Jana blew the kid a kiss. "No one could forget you, Jose."

Witt took that as his cue to head out. But the vision of Jana blowing kisses lingered in his mind the whole drive home.

She didn't notice it at first.

Jana wasn't exactly a morning glory— more like the kind who crawled to the coffeepot in a subhuman state—but she always gave the truck a quick glance out the window when she got up. She could see the truck's designated parking space from her apartment, and she started her day with a glance at it, a nonverbal "good morning" as she shuffled down the small hallway Friday morning toward her kitchen.

Jana stopped, a foot or so past the window, something registering as vaguely off in her sleep-fogged brain. She was so weary from the past few days that she didn't trust her eyes not to play tricks on her.

Rubbing her eyes, she backtracked and looked out again. Her whole body startled awake, jolted out of drowsiness by the scrawl of black spray paint across the side of the bright blue truck.

"Dead Meat." Large, unsteady letters filled the side of the truck next to the counter window. This was no artful graffiti. These were violent, threatening words.

Jana blinked and felt her head spin. She leaned against the wall for a moment, willing the black letters to disappear as a trick of her tired eyes. They didn't. She shook her head again, feeling as if the air had been sucked out of the apartment in the past few seconds. It took her a minute or so to remember where her cell phone was, but when she recalled it was charging on the kitchen counter, she practically ran to the spot and hit Witt's name on her contact screen. She closed her eyes as the phone rang, but the words hung there in front of her eyes, white against the black of her closed lids like a surreal photonegative of what she'd just seen.

"Jana?" Witt's voice sounded as sleepy as she had been moments ago—after all, they'd seen some late nights and he'd driven all the way back to Martins Gap after many of them.

"You need to get here. Now."

"Why?" He was yawning. "Is everything okay?"

"No," she shot back, her throat tight with the threat of frightened tears. "It's not. Someone's…someone's done something to the truck."

She could hear him sit up. Had she woken him? It didn't really matter now. "Done what?"

Jana walked back to the window, half hoping she'd find the brilliant blue unscarred by the ugly letters. "Someone has spray-painted words across the side of the truck." She didn't even want to give the words voice—it felt as if that would make them more real.

"Words?"

Jana turned from the window, leaning back against the wall with her hand over her eyes.

"Someone spray-painted 'Dead Meat' across the side of our truck."

She heard Witt stand up, heard his voice pitch and jerk as he grabbed clothes and whatever else he needed to come out to her. "Are you all right? Nothing's happened to you? Your place?"

She didn't even want to think about the writer of those words getting any closer to her than the truck. "No. At least I don't think so. I should probably open my apartment door and go look, but—"

"No, don't do that. Don't you open that door for anyone but me or the police. Call them right now. I'm in Martins Gap, so I'll be there in forty minutes. And I'll call Nash to see if he can come, as well. He's had some experience with this kind of stuff back when he was a cop in LA. Don't go check on the truck. Don't even look at it if you don't want to. You stay put until we get to you, understand?"

The urgency in Witt's voice unwound the little knot of control she'd been holding. "Okay," she said, her voice soft and wavering.

"Jana?"

"Yeah?"

"It's probably just some stupid kid. A misguided vegetarian with a spray can. Try not to worry. Call the police the minute you hang up with me, okay?"

"I'll do that." She wanted to sound confident, like this hadn't rattled her. She hated how much fear colored her voice.

"It doesn't matter that it's sitting in your parking lot. That truck is Blue Thorn land. And at the Blue Thorn, we protect our own."

We protect our own. The words resonated in Jana's chest like a church bell, deep and powerful. She wanted to find a blue bandanna and clutch it to her chest. To wrap her whole apartment in a shield of blue bandannas. She wanted to believe that the loyalty and protection of the Buckton family surrounded her, but the clutch of fear that bound her chest kept yelling, *You can't have that. Not you.*

"I meant what I said in my note, Jana. You're one of us. We'll protect you."

She knew he wasn't talking about the truck. Witt's voice told her he took this matter personally. She could no longer deny that he took *her* personally, and she didn't know what to do with that. She didn't want to hang up the phone. She wanted Witt to stay on the line with her until he walked in that door—which was foolish, sentimental and from a practical standpoint impossible if she was going to call the police.

"I'll be there soon," he said softly, as if he could tell she needed encouragement to end the call. "I promise."

"Okay." Why couldn't she think of any other response than that? "I'm calling the police now."

Jana ended the call, took a deep breath, and then began pushing the drastic numbers 9-1-1 on her cell. Her finger hovered over the dial button, reluctant to place the call. She'd have to talk about Ronnie. She'd seen enough cop shows to know someone was going to ask her if she knew of anyone who would want to hurt her, and they wouldn't be talking about bad reviews like Spatula Dave. Even the remotest possibility—because that's what it was, the remotest of remote possibilities— that this was Ronnie set off cannons in Jana's stomach.

All the photos, all the publicity. Marion. The social media could easily have been picked up by well-meaning friends and colleagues and made its way back to Atlanta. Back to Ronnie. The possibility wasn't nearly as remote as she wanted to believe.

Jana stared at the phone in her hand. To tell someone about Ronnie Taylor, to speak his name and suggest him as a threat, felt like it gave him life. As if it pulled him back out of the past shadows and opened some unseen door to let him waltz into her all-too-wonderful present. Witt would have to know about him. *Everyone* would have to know about him. The worst mistake of her old life—the sour relationship with a man who thought love was ownership—would have to take up residence in the here and now. That felt blacker than the two words scrawled out there on the truck.

The slow boom of cannons in her gut twisted up into a chatter like machine guns as she pressed the call button and put the phone to her ear.

"Austin Police dispatch. What is the nature of your emergency?"

Jana hadn't thought through how to explain it. Jitters blanked out all the words in her brain. "My truck…the food truck I work at… has been vandalized. Or more. I don't know if it's more than just words spray-painted on the outside. I don't think I should go out there and check it."

"No. Stay away from the scene if you're not there now. But you can see it? Is the person vandalizing it right now?"

Suddenly this didn't feel like a real emergency. She should have dialed the nonemergency number. Lives weren't at stake here.

"No." She pushed her hair out of her eyes, feeling overdramatic. Witt had said to call the police, not 9-1-1. "They're gone. At least I think they're gone. I mean, I woke up to find 'Dead Meat' spray-painted on the side. I can see the truck from my apartment window."

"The truck is near you?"

Jana gave her address and described the corner of the parking lot where the truck sat, as though a vividly blue food truck wouldn't stand out among the sedans and hatchbacks.

"Is there anyone inside? Could anyone be hurt?"

It was far too early for Jose to be there. She'd have to call him and tell him to stay away until they got this mess cleared up—if Witt hadn't already thought of it. How could they get the ugly words off fast enough to open back up for business? Did whoever did this know tomorrow was the rodeo finals? Were they seeking to disable the Blue Thorn truck or just to rattle her cage? Did it matter? They'd done both. "I don't think anyone could be hurt," she replied, now pacing the hall in front of the window. "No one should be in the truck, and I can't even tell if he got inside or not." He? Did she have any right to say 'he' when she didn't know for sure who had done this? "Right now all I can see is the spray paint. No one is in danger right now that I can see."

"Well, that's good. Stay put, keep an eye on the truck and an officer will be over there soon. He's going to look at the truck first and then come to your apartment. Are you alone where you are?"

Jana was comfortable with her own company, and enjoyed the quiet of solitude away from the hustle of the kitchen. This morning, she felt the small apartment echo enormous and empty around her. "I am."

"Lock your door if it isn't already. If you like I can stay on the line with you until you see the squad car in the parking lot."

That felt silly. She was in no real danger. She was hundreds of feet from the truck and whoever had painted the message was long gone. "No," she said. "I'm fine."

Nothing could be further from the truth.

Chapter Fourteen

Witt made the forty-minute drive in twenty-seven heart-pounding minutes. Austin traffic was notorious, so he'd taken every back-road shortcut he knew and broken more speed limits than his soon-to-be cousin-in-law Nash could ever condone, even under these circumstances.

He'd held it together until the text from Jana came. Police on the way, she'd written, then added a photo of the truck. It was fuzzy and from the high angle of her apartment window, but even so he could read the slash of jagged letters spelling "Dead Meat" across the panel beside the customer windows. At that point the safety valve came off Witt's conscience and he'd floored the car the rest of the way, praying for safety, wisdom and an absence of police speed guns.

He paused to stare at the truck for only for a sick handful of seconds before taking the stairs to Jana's floor at a run, unwilling to wait for the slow elevator.

Jana looked rattled—something he'd never seen before. The tense look in her eyes as she answered the door dug into his chest, hinting at something that had been seeping into him the entire drive: Jana was more to him than just an employee. He hadn't once thought of this incident in terms of someone threatening Blue Thorn Burgers—it had only ever felt like someone out to harm *Jana*. And that was a thought he could barely stand.

He pulled her into his arms. The act likely crossed a dozen professional boundaries, but he didn't care. She looked frightened and he wanted to protect her. It had made him crazy that he wasn't here for her when she saw the truck.

Jana put up no resistance, clinging to him fiercely. At least for the minute or two before she seemed to regain her composure. "You're here," she said with an air of relief that went straight through him.

"I came as fast as I could. I reckon I broke one or six speeding laws on the way after I saw that photograph."

"You might want to keep that to yourself,"

Jana said, trying to smile as she nodded her head behind her to where Witt could now see a police officer sitting at her kitchen counter. "Come on in."

Jana introduced Witt to Sergeant Ed Nichols, a friendly guy who seemed to be taking this attack seriously. Nash had warned him that a big-city police department might shrug this off as just graffiti.

"Miss Powers tells me you're the owner of the truck?" Sergeant Nichols asked, adding to a list of notes on a yellow legal pad.

"I am."

"I'll need you to sign the formal complaint seeing as it's your property. I think we need to investigate this as much as a threat as vandalism, given the words on your truck out there. Miss Powers gave me the keys and I looked inside, but nothing seems to be out of order there. So this was more message than destruction, I'd say."

Witt sat down, glad for that tiny bit of good news but still stunned with worry. "I agree."

"Aside from what Miss Powers has told me, and the other rodeo finalists, can you think of anyone who might want to rattle your cage right now? Competitors, disgruntled former employees, that sort of thing?"

"No one associated with the truck. The

ranch has made a few enemies over the years, but that's quite a way from here." Witt told a quick version of the Blue Thorn Ranch's battle with an upscale developer last spring, and the shooting of some bison earlier this year. "I suppose it could be related, but it's hard to see how." None of the other finalists would stoop this low, would they?

Nichols wrote a few lines. "Best to think of all possibilities. I'd like you to make a list of former ranch employees, anyone who was involved in that real estate business you just mentioned and the kids who did that shooting. I'll add it to the name Miss Powers has given me and we'll start there."

The name Jana had given him? Witt raised an eyebrow at Jana, who was now chewing on her fingernails and not meeting his gaze. What was going on here? What didn't he know?

"I'll have an evidence technician out within the hour. When he's done, you'll be cleared to do whatever you need to in order to clean that up. I'm sure you want that message off your truck as soon as possible."

"We can't open with that on there," Jana said, her voice unsteady.

Witt hadn't even thought about the commercial ramifications of a vandalized truck—

particularly with the message currently on it. "No," he replied quietly. "But we can get it taken care of. Maybe even today. I've got Nash sending me the name of someone who can clean it off, or paint over it." Nash had a passion for classic cars, and knew plenty of garages in the area.

He'd hoped the prospect of making those words go away would take the shadows out from under her eyes, but it didn't change much. Witt stood up as Sergeant Nichols closed his notebook, handing the officer a card. "Anything you need from us, anything at all, please call."

"You can count on it," the sergeant said. "If it's any help, Miss Powers, a few of the guys at the station know your truck. And your burgers. Good stuff, they say. They'll put in the extra mile for you, I reckon."

Witt didn't know if tasty burgers meant better police protection, but he'd take any advantage he could get right now. "Catch the creep," Witt offered as he walked the officer to the door, "and we'll come feed the force some Friday night on the house."

"Not necessary," Nichols said, "but I'll pass along the word just the same. You'll both be hearing from me this afternoon if not within the next few hours. I'll have the evidence technician call up here before he goes near the truck. He may want to go inside."

"Sure," Jana said flatly.

Witt saw the officer out, locking the door behind him. It struck him, as he turned the key in the deadbolt, that this was the first time he'd been in Jana's apartment. What lousy circumstances to be seeing her place. He wanted to look around, to see what kind of living space she'd made for herself, but that would have to wait until later. Right now there was only one question he wanted to ask.

As he sat back down at the table opposite Jana, she looked at him with resignation, as if she was waiting for him to ask.

"Sergeant Nichols said you gave him a name."

"I did," she said, spreading her hands on the placemat in front of her where a cup of coffee sat untouched.

"That sounds pretty specific to me." Witt wanted to reach for one of those hands flattened against the table, but stopped himself. "Do you know who did this, Jana?"

She kept her eyes on the table even as he tried to dip his head into her view. He'd never felt such a distance from her, and after the hug at the doorway the space between them now gaped vast and cold.

"Jana?"

"Maybe…" Her voice was so soft—it didn't sound like the Jana he knew.

He placed his hand over hers even as he told himself not to. "Tell me. I don't understand why you didn't tell me before, but tell me now."

"His name is Ronnie Taylor." Witt watched her drag the words up from somewhere deep down, a place she clearly dreaded revisiting. "We were…together…in culinary school and just after. He… Well, he's an intense kind of guy. At first I liked it—all the charisma and power. The grand romantic gestures. The way he looked at me as if I were the most important thing in the world."

Witt didn't like where this was heading. He felt the hand on Jana's tighten up, and forced himself to loosen his grip. Rather than reply or urge her on, he felt it was best to stay silent, pray for control and let her unwind the story at her own pace.

"Then it became more and more about Ronnie being the most important thing in *my* world. He'd get miffed if I spent time with other people. He began to put down my cooking when it started to gain attention. He was in sales—commercial ovens, refrigeration systems, that sort of thing—and the part of my career that he loved at first began to bother him. He didn't like my staying out with friends after work." Jana looked up at him with wounded eyes. "You know how these things go. This isn't a new story. I thank God every day I got out from underneath him and away. Lots of women don't, you know."

Witt's stomach turned cold. He couldn't believe he was about to ask this question. "Did he hurt you?"

The pause before she answered turned his gut to ice. "Not physically." She gave the thinnest of sighs. "Let's just say Ronnie didn't need my knife set to know how to cut deep."

"Jana." What was there to say to something like that? It made him want to put his fist through a wall. "I'm so sorry." The words seemed miles from useful, but he couldn't think of anything else to say.

"You and me both." She pulled her hand from his and hugged herself. "Ronnie was a huge mistake. I wanted him to stay forever in my past. Act as if he never existed."

"That's why you didn't tell me."

Jana nodded rather than replying. For a woman who'd never once shied away from telling him what she thought, he found her silence heartbreaking. "And here I go plastering your face all over Austin, doing my level best to make sure everybody knows who you are." He stood up to pace the kitchen, all the tension and anger of the past hours boiling over. "I'm an idiot," he groaned, flailing his hands through the air because it felt like the only thing that would keep him from punching something. "I shouldn't have pushed you into a relentless, stupid PR campaign. I've just set you out there like a target for a creep like him."

"It's not your fault." Her words were so quiet, so lifeless. Not at all like the Jana who'd fascinated him for weeks now.

"Yes, it is my fault. You told me you didn't want photos of yourself, only the food. You told me we weren't ready for the rodeo contest that would only put you out there more. You tried to stop me, and I didn't listen. And now there's some jerk out there looking to..." He sat back down across from her and grabbed her hands, both of them, no matter how many lines it crossed. "Please say you forgive me for bringing this on you. If I'd have known..."

That sparked something in her eyes. She shot out of her chair, hands slipping from his grasp. "If you'd have known, you wouldn't have done what's best for the truck. Or Blue Thorn. And, okay, maybe for my career, too." She turned to him. "And that lets Ronnie win. That lets him control my life just like he wanted to, don't you see? He doesn't get to win. I won't let him. I won't act as if he can do anything to control me or the choices I make, because he can't." She practically spit the last words out, the glimmer of tears threatening in her wide eyes.

He hated his response, but it had to be said. "But Jana, there are still things he can do to hurt you. He might be doing them right now." He stood up and came around to her side of the table. "If he's here, threatening you, we have to face it. And I mean *we*, because I will not let you do this alone. I'm going to be right beside you until this whole mess is cleared up. If you have to face Ronnie, I promise you right now, you will not face him alone."

She looked up at him for a long, fragile moment. Witt watched her eyes fill with tears, her lip quiver even as she bit it. She seemed frozen there, on the edge of her composure, trying so hard to hang on. He felt himself falling in that last-ditch moment, watching her let go of the fierce independence he'd once found so compelling.

When she crumpled against him, the long-held-back sob warm and wet against his chest, he felt his heart leave him and wrap itself around her. He'd meant his promise moments ago, but now he felt it pulse through his veins like a vow. He would not let her go through this alone.

"Darlin', I'm so glad you're okay!" Adele Buckton pulled Jana into a hug that was surprisingly fierce given the woman's advanced age. "I can't believe anyone would do such a thing. You must be shaking in your boots."

"I'm okay," Jana replied, half meaning it. While some part of her wanted to stand her ground in Austin, a larger part of her quickly agreed with Witt that getting out of the city was a better idea. At least for the day. "The contest people were great about letting me out of today's interviews. Even though I'm sure they thought it might make for an enticing headline."

"*No one* gets to exploit this," Witt declared, taking the overnight bag she'd quickly packed and setting it on the porch. "Whoever did this wants exposure, and I'm going to make sure he never gets it."

"Nash will make sure that truck looks good as new when you get back to it, hon. He shot out of here like a man on a mission. He and Jose will take care of it, you rest assured." She looked at Witt. "I think even your buddy Mark is lending a hand."

Jana cringed a bit at all the fuss. "Nash is busy with his new job as sheriff, and the wedding and all."

Adele scowled. "He's not one bit too busy to help out with something like this." Adele kept one arm around Jana's shoulder and pulled her toward the kitchen. "I don't know what the world's coming to anymore."

"Thank you for having me out," Jana repeated.

"Well, Witt wouldn't stand for you sitting around in that apartment with all that's gone on, and it's not as if you can take the truck anywhere until it's cleaned up." She steered Jana to the kitchen's large wooden table. "If Witt hadn't asked, I would have offered anyway. Now, you sit here while I get some tea going. Chicken salad is waiting in the fridge."

Gunner's wife, Brooke, came into the room with a bright-eyed infant in her arms. "Hi, Jana. I heard about the truck. I can't believe someone would do that. It's terrible."

"Jana, you remember my cousin Gunner's wife and their boy, Trey?" Witt asked as he took a large crockery bowl out of the fridge.

"How is the little guy?" Jana asked as Trey wobbled a chubby hand in her direction.

"Growing fast. He'll be running before he walks, I expect."

Adele laughed. "I don't think Gunner ever sat down from the moment he figured out how to walk. The boy was his own tiny stampede. Even between his mama, Gunner Senior, Grandpa and I, we could barely contain him."

Witt set the bowl and a stack of bread slices in the middle of the table. "So not much has changed, huh, Gran?"

That brought a laugh from both Adele and Brooke. Jana forced a smile, glad to be here amongst such warmth but still a long way from calm.

They groped their way into a pleasant, chatty lunch. Jana couldn't tell if they were keeping the conversation deliberately light for her sake, or if life was just that easy and simple out here on the ranch. It didn't matter—the good basic food, the distance from Austin and the warm family dynamic calmed her spirit. When Adele shooed her and Witt outside onto the porch swing while she cleaned up from lunch and Trey went down for his nap, Jana didn't put up an argument. She felt ready to nap herself.

"Vandalism is exhausting," she said as she settled into the swing with the afghan Adele had given her. She waited to see where Witt would sit. They hadn't talked about how she'd ended up in his arms back at the apartment, but she knew by the careful way they maneuvered around each other now that it was on both their minds.

He sat on the coffee table right in front of the swing, directly across from her and close—but not too close. Parking his elbows on his knees and leaning in, he asked, "How are you? Now, I mean?"

She pulled her knees up under the knitted throw, feeling the swing sway lazily from her shift of weight. "Better. You're right. I'd have been a mess just bumping around the apartment today."

Witt craned his neck to look out at the pastures. "It's only a forty-minute drive, but it's a whole other world out here. Best getaway there is." He looked down for a moment, weaving his fingers together. "I'm pulling us from the finals."

Jana sat up. "No."

His eyes found hers. "We don't need the prize money—we'll succeed without it. Nothing's worth what just happened."

She swung her legs down so that she was facing him. "I've been afraid Ronnie would show back up in my life for years. Terrified of how I'd feel if he did. And now he has—

or may have—and yes, I'm scared. But I'm also ready to fight back."

The breeze blew strands of curls in her eyes, and she pushed them back. "I let him take too much from me before. I'm not that scared young girl anymore." She surprised herself by reaching for Witt's arm. "I'm the chef at Blue Thorn Burgers, and Ronnie Taylor does not get to take that from me. Or from you and your family. He's one guy and you're a whole big strong family. You said it yourself—I'm not alone in this. So let's act like it."

"But we missed today's events," Witt countered. "And I don't know how we or the truck will manage to be ready in time. Look, we've already made it to the finals. We've made our mark and people know who we are. We even got Dave's publicity. We'll be fine. We don't need to win. I don't want to risk your safety."

"I don't want to bow out—not if we can get the truck ready. I don't care about the grant or the other prizes—you just said yourself that we'll expand on our own because we're that good. I don't need to prove to anyone that I can cook. I *do* need to prove to myself that Ronnie has no hold over me. And I do that by staying in the game. By showing up at those finals tomorrow night."

"I want you protected. I want whoever did

that to you and the truck to get caught and punished. And if it's Ronnie, I want to catch the creep and keep him away from you for good," Witt added.

She sat back again, unnerved by the powerful determination in Witt's eyes. "Well, yes, that, too."

"And I don't know if we can do that with you in the middle of all those people tomorrow night." Witt leaned forward and took hold of her hand. "Look at you. You're shaking. That alone makes me want to pummel this guy."

Jana let him hold her hand. She needed his touch and his words right now, professional margins or no. She'd been fighting this shadow for so many years on her own, and it was like a lifeline to have someone else fighting beside her. To know the whole Buckton family had her back. She'd managed to scrape up confidence over the years, but this was the closest thing to safe she'd felt in a long time. "I don't want to let him take this from me," she said softly, wiping away the tear that slid down her cheek. She really, really didn't want to cry in front of Witt again, but she wasn't sure she could stop the tears now that they had come.

"Hey, hold on there…" Witt said, moving

from the table to slide onto the swing beside her. He wrapped his arms and the afghan around her, and she let him. She didn't stop herself from sinking against his warm chest and feeling the solidness of his arms as they held her. "Nobody's going to let this jerk take anything from you. You wear the blue bandanna, and the Blue Thorn takes care of its own. If we can handle big, angry bison, then we can handle one cowardly sneak with a can of spray paint."

"You're a good boss, you know that?" She sniffed into his shoulder, feeling like it was right to shove the word *boss* in between them right now before things went any further.

"I'm not talking as your boss right now, Jana." He tapped her head, making her look up at him. She knew she was lost when she did, for the look in his eyes seemed to go right through her. There wasn't any hope of hiding what had grown between them at that point. Whether it made business sense or not hardly mattered. "I'm talking as your…friend," he said, the hesitation speaking volumes. After a moment, he leaned in, and Jana was half delighted, half terrified he was going to kiss her. He left a soft kiss on her cheek, and she felt herself dissolve under the tenderness. "As someone who…cares about you."

She didn't even realize that her hand had lifted to the spot where he'd kissed her until she followed his gaze. "Witt..." She knew she ought to draw the line right here, to say what dangerous territory that kiss was, but she couldn't make the words come out.

"Yeah," he said softly, touching her hand as it lay against her cheek. "We're going to have to figure out what to do about that. But not now."

"We really can't." She managed to get the words out, but they tasted sour on her tongue.

"Part of me knows that," he said, standing up and running his hands through his hair. She wanted to call him back to the swing, to spend a few more minutes in that safe place inside his arms. "Another part of me isn't so sure."

Chapter Fifteen

"I can't believe someone did that," the contest official said, looking genuinely upset and concerned. "I'd delay the finals if I could, but it's not possible."

"I understand that, but we don't want to pull out," Witt said. "With your cooperation and the help from the police department, we're going to stay in. We don't want to give this creep what he wants, which is obviously to spook us out of the finals."

"Who would do such a thing?" The official looked around the park that had been set up like a triangle with the Blue Thorn truck, the Frostings truck and TexTaco truck on each side, with a cluster of voting kiosks in the middle. "You don't think it's either of them, do you?" she said as she nodded to the two other trucks. "I just can't see them doing something like that, even to win."

"No, we think we have an idea of who it is," Witt said. "You'll understand that I can't say any more than that."

"Of course. We'll do everything we can to help tonight."

"There will be several plainclothes policemen around the truck in addition to the guys in uniform around the park."

Jana walked up to them, looking shaky but determined. "Hi, Val," she greeted the contest coordinator. "Nice bit of drama, huh?"

"It's despicable. I'm so sorry you have to go through this."

Jana pulled an envelope from her pocket. "Well, maybe tonight will be the last of it. I wanted to give you this." She produced a stack of color-copied photographs and handed several to Val and one to Witt. "It's an old photo, but not that old. It's someone from my past who may be doing this, trying to make trouble. If you see him, tell security right away."

Witt hadn't known she was going to do this. It seemed both wise and dangerous at the same time. He knew how much she hated to bring her past out into the open, and his admiration of her doubled at the courage she was showing right now. Witt stared at the picture of Ronnie's face, feeling a surge of hate for the guy and what he'd done to Jana. If he saw that face tonight, he couldn't honestly say he wouldn't take the guy down with his own bare hands.

"This is supposed to be your victory night," he said to Jana, "not the showdown at the food truck corral." The joke fell desperately short. Witt sent up his hundredth prayer of the night for God to watch over Jana, over all of them.

"Maybe it still will be," Jana said, her smile forced and thin.

Val leaned in. "I'm not supposed to play favorites, but I hope you end tonight with the guy behind bars and a big fat grant in your hands."

"Thank you," Jana and Witt said at the same time. Witt wanted to win tonight, but it wasn't for any of the reasons he'd thought of when he'd entered Blue Thorn in the contest. It wasn't for any reasons that involved him, actually. He wanted it for Jana. He wanted tonight to launch her out of the self-imposed shadow she had hid behind for years, to let her vibrancy come out in all its glory, for her to be the woman God clearly intended her to be but who Ronnie had stolen from her.

Still, none of that would be worth risking her safety. For as much as he'd placed on the line for Blue Thorn Burgers, it astonished him how easily he would pull the plug on the whole thing if it meant keeping Jana safe. He grabbed her hand as they walked back to the truck. "We can shut this whole thing down in a heartbeat if you don't feel safe."

He could tell the words surprised her as much as they did him. He'd changed in the months running the truck, and they both knew it. She'd changed as well, but the biggest transformation had been inside him. Could she see it as much as he felt it? Did she realize how much of it was because of her?

A warm gush of gratitude—and yes, affection—glowed in her eyes. "No, I don't feel safe. Not completely. But I feel protected, and that's close enough." She squeezed his hand, and he felt it rush though him in something much warmer than a tingle. "I want to keep in this. I don't want to back out." She managed a telling smile. "But I want you in that truck, right behind me, the whole time. If I see him, I want to know you're right there."

"My parents are here." Witt didn't know what made him say that. It didn't add to Jana's protection—and then again, it did. "My mom brought her whole church women's group up.

They're all going to get burgers and vote, and they're going to pray over the truck to keep you safely inside." He hadn't meant to share that bit—it felt churchy and dramatic. Then again, if tonight wasn't a time to draw on the power of prayer, when was?

Jana's eyes glistened. She was clearly touched by the gesture. "Witt, that's so sweet." She gave him a knowing look, seemingly aware of the weight of her next comment. "Your dad is here?"

"Yeah," he replied gruffly, at a loss for how to convey the torrent of emotions his father's presence stirred up. "Imagine that, huh?" Witt's heart expanded in gratitude and twisted in defensiveness all at the same time—not a recipe for the calm thinking he needed tonight.

"He should be proud of his son tonight, no matter how we place."

Witt stopped walking, struck by the words. "I hope so." In that one wish, Jana had managed to capture the yearning that'd been tumbling around his chest for weeks. The basic, bone-deep need for a son to feel his father's pride in him. He'd let Cole steal that from him in the same way Jana had let Ronnie steal her confidence. *Tonight*, he prayed as he walked toward the truck, keeping Jana's hand in his, *let all of that end*.

Jana stopped just before climbing up into the truck. "I'm proud of us," she said, her smile less forced this time. "I feel like we win no matter what ribbon we earn tonight." Her cheeks pinked then, and the put one hand to her face. "Wow, that sounded cheesy." She looked at him. "You know what I mean."

Witt brushed a lock of curls from her cheek, pleased by what his touch did to her eyes. Someday, when this was all over, maybe he'd let himself kiss more than that cheek. Jana was beautiful. Strong and courageous and inventive and talented. He would be kidding himself if he tried to believe their partnership hadn't already gone much deeper than burgers and coleslaw. "Soul mate"—perhaps one of the cheesiest terms of all time in Witt's opinion—suddenly didn't seem overdramatic.

Jose's bike skidded to a stop behind Witt. "Are you ready to win this thing?" the boy asked, one fist in the air. Then his mouth fell open, and Witt realized his hand was still on Jana's cheek. "Whoa. No kidding?"

It would have been a better choice to react with a casual calm, as if they didn't have anything to hide, but Jana practically jumped away from Witt. "I…I had something on my cheek."

"Yeah," Jose said, a smirk on his face, "Witt's hand." Jose swung off his bike and pointed at Witt. "Slick move, Señor Buckton." He said the words with such a teasing, sing-song tone that Witt felt his own face redden.

"It's not…"

Jose threw up his hands. "Don't go there, dude. Ain't no big deal to me."

"Jose," Jana started.

"Hey, Chef, I just clean up around here. It's no business of mine whose hand is tenderly caressing your cheek." He said the last words as if they were ballad song lyrics, and Witt fought the urge to cuff the back of Jose's head.

"Can we all just start cooking?" Jana threw out in an exasperated tone as she climbed into the truck.

"Oh, I think someone already started cook—"

"Enough!" Witt cut him off with a bark, meeting Jose's ridiculous grin with the darkest look he could manage.

"Yes, boss," Jose replied, but not before offering Witt a wink that made him regret ever hiring the boy.

The truck needed to be three times its present size to hold all the things going on within its walls tonight. *Pray hard, Mom. We're gonna need it.*

Keep me cooking, Lord, just keep me cooking. Every few orders, Jana would look up to the verse from Jeremiah she had tacked up above the grill:

"For I know the plans I have for you," declares the Lord, "plans to prosper you and not to harm you, plans to give you hope and a future."

She knew the verse by heart, but somehow seeing the words in solid form over the window that looked out onto the crowd gave her extra assurance.

"Hi, Miss Jana!" Audie's pigtails bounced as the little girl jumped up to peek into the truck window. "We're here to eat and vote. Even Trey—but he only gets a french fry."

Jana smiled. "Your usual?" Audie had become a big fan of the Blue Thorn kid's meal.

"Two. I brought a friend from school so she can vote, too."

"Coming right up," Jana replied as she added a pair of slider burgers to the grill. She accepted a long, encouraging look from

Audie's mom, Brooke. Jana couldn't begin
to know how to repay the family for turning
up in full force to show their support. Ellic
and Nash were there, too, Nash in his sheriff's uniform and clearly on guard as they
mingled around the truck. "Gran's at home,"
Ellie had said, "but she's got her whole church
group praying." Jana began to feel stronger,
bolstered by the support of all the Bucktons.
If Ronnie were to try anything tonight, he'd
meet with a full-scale Buckton defense.

The next half hour passed without incident,
with happy customers offering praise for Blue
Thorn Burgers. Even if they didn't win, the
number of new customers they had won over
in the competition was prize enough. Witt
was right; tonight truly was the launch of a
new life for Jana. She couldn't remember a
time when she'd felt so smack-dab in the middle of where God created her to be.

She was offering a bustling prayer of praise
for that confidence—thanksgiving flowing
out of her like breath as she moved through
the actions of cooking for so many—when a
pair of sharp thuds hit the side of the truck.
Cries of alarm rang out from the people
standing in line, stepping back and pointing
as two more thuds pounded. With horror, Jana
saw red splatter the arm of a young woman as

she screamed. As she peered out the counter window, something whizzed past her ear to land with an angry burst on the wall behind her, red spraying everywhere.

Witt grabbed her, pulling her down as two more shots sailed through the counter window to burst on the back wall, filling the cabin with red splatters.

From the floor, Jana heard cries from outside the truck rise above the pounding in her ears. Her lungs seized until her vision started to blacken around the edges. She watched a thick red rivulet run down the truck wall, and wondered numbly if she'd been hit.

"Blood?" she gasped, unable to make any sense of the chaos unfolding around her.

Three more hits pounded the outside of the truck, and Jana had the gruesome vision of the truck being covered in splatters of blood. Dead Meat indeed. She clung to Witt, burying her face in his chest where she could feel his own heart pounding a mile a minute and his breath coming in frantic pants.

"It's paint," he said, and she lifted her head to see his red-smeared hand holding a shredded white orb. "Paint balls, filled with red paint—not blood."

A rapid-fire succession of hits pounded the truck, three more flying through the counter window before Jose, letting out a stream of angry Spanish, grabbed the counter window and yanked it down. The outside shouts were muffled a bit now, leaving the three of them gasping at each other, shocked but unharmed. Red slid down the back wall in sickening drips, pooling on the floor all too much like wounds.

Jana heard yells and sirens but didn't move. Witt went to stand but she wouldn't let him, clinging to him in a desperate panic that refused to subside.

"We're okay," he said, turning his head around to take in all of the truck. "Jose, you okay?"

"I'm not hurt. Scared out of my wits, maybe, but not hurt. Man, what was that?"

Jana knew. It settled in her bones with an icy certainty. "That was Ronnie."

"This Ronnie is a sick dude. Why does he want to kill you?" Jose asked.

The words hit her as sharply as one of the projectiles. *Does he want to kill me?*

"Scare, more likely," Witt said, starting to stand again.

"It worked." Jana spat the words out, her fear now mixing with anger. "On me and all our customers."

The back door of the truck burst open,

making Jana jump. She was sure it was Ronnie coming in to finish what he'd started.

Instead, it was Nash, panting and smeared in some of the red paint himself. "We got him," he said as his eyes flew around the spattered cabin. "You all okay in here?"

"'Okay' might be a reach," Witt replied, suddenly noticing the large smear of red down his arm. He grabbed a towel from the counter and began wiping it off. "Unharmed, yes. Okay? Well, that might take a bit."

Nash was standing in front of Jana, but she still felt as if she'd fall over any second. "Did you hear me, Jana? We got him. We got Ronnie. He was firing from a tree at the edge of the park but we got him."

"Is anyone hurt? Outside, I mean?" Jana heard Witt ask, sounding as if he were a thousand miles away. Her head was swimming and she stood looking at her shaking, red-splattered hands. Even though she knew it was paint, she looked bloody. Wounded.

"No one was hurt. The only real damage is to the truck—plus he gave everyone a good scare, which is what he wanted, I guess. The weasel. He's under arrest, no doubt about that."

Jana was still staring at her hands when she watched Witt wrap them in a dish towel and tenderly begin wiping them off. "Did you hear that, Jana? He's under arrest. He can't bother you now. It's over."

She looked up into Witt's eyes, finding such kindness in them. She ought to say something, but every word seemed out of reach. Witt took the towel and wiped her cheek—the same spot where his hand had brushed earlier. "You're okay. We're all okay."

A policeman and the event organizer poked their heads into the back door of the truck. "Everybody all right in here?"

"All okay," Nash replied. "The crowd?"

"Shaken, but no panic. I'm going to make an announcement over the PA system in a minute. The event's got another two hours scheduled—we're going to try to stay open if possible."

Witt shifted into gear. "Clear a path and we'll get this truck out of here."

"I think that's best," the officer said.

"I'll take Jana to my cruiser," Nash said. He turned to address her and Witt. "We can get a full statement in the morning so right now you all can get away from this."

"We'll lose." Jana listened to the words come crisp and cold like a certain, sure fact.

Witt took her face in his hands. "Do you think I care about that right now?" His eyes were like beacons, the one clear thing she could focus on while the red paint seemed to smear everything else in sight. "Go with Nash. I'll make sure my folks are okay, get the truck out of here and meet you at the ranch. Witt looked at Nash. "No reporters, no photos, no attention."

"Absolutely," Nash assured. Jose had somehow gathered up her belongings—including a freshly ironed chef's coat she had planned to wear to accept whatever prize they would win tonight. She'd kept it tucked away where it wouldn't get spattered with grease, and it was the only thing in the truck not smeared with red. "Come with me, Jana," Nash said in quiet, comforting tones. "I'll take care of you while Witt takes care of the truck."

She told herself not to turn, not to look. She didn't want to see what the outside of the truck looked like, didn't want to hold another image of the now beloved blue truck vandalized by Ronnie's ongoing hate. Only she seemed powerless not to look. The sight of the truck, covered in angry red stains like a blood-soaked battlefield, felt as if it would linger in her mind forever.

Chapter Sixteen

"I still can't believe it all happened," Ellie said, bringing Jana a glass of orange juice as she sat down at the ranch house kitchen table the next morning. "Right in front of us. It was like watching something out of a movie."

"No movie I'd want to see," Jana said. She wondered when the skittish, look-over-her-shoulder feeling would subside. Being at the ranch helped, but Jana still hated how Ronnie could rattle her nerves even from behind bars.

"I hate to think of you having to live with that fear alone for all those years. Were you going through this even when we worked together at GoodEats?"

Jana pushed one curl off her forehead—the rest were tied back in a Blue Thorn bandanna. It was foolish, but Jana felt as if she wanted to keep one of those turquoise squares on her body for the next year as a visual reminder that she was now safe. "It had all just happened when you and I met. I really thought the worst of it was over. He bothered me a few times at GoodEats, but mostly late-night phone calls or annoying texts. I think I convinced myself he'd moved on. I was wrong on that score, wasn't I?" She took a long sip of tea. "Have you heard from Nash?"

"This morning, early. He went back to Austin last night seeing to the case after he dropped you off. Witt should be here soon—he was seeing to getting that awful stuff off the truck this morning." Ellie looked at Jana. "I've never seen Witt so worked up. Even with all that business about Cole, he was never like this."

"He loves that truck," Jana replied, rubbing her eyes. It had taken her forever to fall asleep last night and she'd woken this morning feeling as if she'd run a marathon. She needed Witt close. She knew he had to be the one to drive the truck out of there that night, but a part of her wouldn't settle until he returned to her side. She'd fallen for him, and hard.

Ellie stared. "It's not about the truck. Come on, you have to know that."

Jana didn't have the strength to put up a front. "Maybe."

Ellie leaned in on both elbows. "Maybe nothing. You have to know how he feels about you, how you feel about him. Even I can see it. Even Jose said something."

Jana shut her eyes. "It's so complicated, Ellie."

"Don't you give me the business about complication. There isn't a relationship on this ranch that isn't complicated." She adopted Miss Adele's broad drawl. "Don't faze us none around here."

"You Bucktons are a complicated bunch, that's for sure."

"Wait until you meet the twins, Luke and Tess. They take Buckton complicated to a whole new level. They're invited to the wedding, of course, but there's no telling if they'll come. And I have every intention of crossing the plus-ones off your invitation and Witt's because you're going together, even if I have to get Nash to handcuff you to each other." Ellie stilled, giving Jana a long look. "It goes both ways, I can see it. You've got it for him like he has it for you."

Jana didn't know how to answer that. She found Witt tremendously attractive. And kind. And driven. She knew that the reason the anxious buzzing hadn't yet left her stomach was because Witt wasn't here. It was his presence that made her feel safe. Even as they'd crouched in the besieged truck with red splattering everywhere, he had made her feel protected. Was that love? Did she even know what love was? Jana felt like she only knew what Ronnie had given her, and that wasn't anything close to love.

Ellie reached for Jana's arm. "Why are you so afraid of what you feel for Witt?"

Jana raised one eyebrow. "Isn't it obvious? He's my boss."

"He's stopped using that word, you know. He calls you his partner. And his eyes just shine when he talks about what you two are going to do with that truck. Oh, sure, it was all 'I's at first—no one can say Witt Buckton doesn't like to make big plans—but it became all 'we' and 'Jana and I' pretty fast."

Partners. Isn't that what she felt, what she'd been feeling for a while now? It was still his signature on her paycheck, but she did feel a link to him that spoke deeply of equality. Jana had too many thoughts tumbling around in her head to make any reply to Ellie, so she simply sipped her juice.

"Do you know what Witt said to Gunner before the finals last night?"

"What?"

"He said—and this is a direct quote here—

'I don't care if we win. I just want to see Jana get the recognition she deserves.'" Ellie sat back. "That's not the Witt I used to know. Don't get me wrong, he's always been a good man. But it was like he spent so much time looking up at the castles he was building in the sky that he'd forget about the rest of us down on the ground. But not anymore. No, sir, that man has changed. Don't you sit there and tell me you have no idea why."

Jana put her head in her hands. "So what am I supposed to do? We don't even know if we have a truck anymore. We don't know how the rodeo went after we left. We don't even know when we'll open up again."

"How about you figure it out together?"

"Me and Witt."

"As partners. And more, unless you're chicken." Ellie leaned in right in front of Jana's face. "And I have never seen anything to make me think Jana Powers is chicken."

Jana pushed her back. "No, I'm mostly burgers."

"Very funny." The gate intercom buzzer went off on the kitchen wall, Witt's voice coming through the crackling speaker.

"It's Witt. I'm here."

Ellie stood up, staring at Jana while she hit

the intercom button. "Okay, Witt. It's Ellie. I'm here in the kitchen with Jana."

"She's okay?"

Ellie winked at Jana, a silent *See what I mean?*

"I'm fine," Jana called out, hoping he could hear her. "Tired, but fine."

"I'll be up to the house in a minute."

The prospect of Witt's appearance made Jana realize just how disheveled she looked. Her face must be a puffy, blotchy mess, and her hair felt like a bird's nest. She didn't want to face Witt looking like this, so even though it pulled just the look she would have expected from Ellie, Jana said, "I think I'm going to go clean up a bit."

"You do that," Ellie said, not tamping down the teasing tone in her voice one single bit. "I'll get our hero some coffee while you freshen up. But don't you be long. He's not here to talk to me."

I know that, Jana thought as she climbed the stairs. *But am I ready to really talk to him?*

As Witt drove up to the ranch house, his whole body seemed to come unwound. The tension from the last twenty-four hours, the constant state of alert he'd been in, had taxed him more than he'd realized. Now that it was over, an oppressive exhaustion seemed to envelop him out of nowhere.

Ronnie Taylor was behind bars, hopefully to never bother Jana again. His brain knew the danger was mostly past, and he was bringing good news to the ranch. His pulse—and, if he was honest with himself, his heart—refused to settle until he set eyes on Jana again. Sending her off with Nash last night had felt like ripping skin off—Witt seemed to sense every mile between them while all this business settled itself. The logical part of him wanted her as far away from Ronnie and the truck as possible. Another part of him needed her close. Needed her, period.

He'd wrested with that need the entire drive out here, mulling, praying, dissecting, analyzing as best he could while he battled the emotional and physical fog that refused to lift. As a guy known for his clear head in a tight spot, this befuddlement was unsettling. Logistically, he was still clear-headed. Emotionally, he was fumbling around in the dark, unsure of his next move.

Halfway to Martins Gap, he'd come to a conclusion. He needed to do what he always did: move forward. Find the next step and take it, ready or not.

Trouble was, he knew what that next step was, and he was the furthest thing from ready to take it. He was pretty sure once he saw Jana, though, the whole of Gunner's herd wouldn't be able to stop him. He needed Jana. Needed to be with Jana, to be close to her, to match his heart to hers despite the whopping risks involved for both of them.

If he did that, he'd have to be all in, fully committed and ready to see it out to the end. She deserved that. She deserved a guy who would put himself 100 percent on the line for her. It was the only way to repair all the damage Ronnie had done. If things went south between him and Jana, there could be no friendship or even professional partnership. This was an all-or-nothing proposition.

This was either the love of his life, or his biggest failure at a time he could least afford to fail.

Funny, he prayed as he turned down the road that led to the Blue Thorn gate, *I thought the truck was my biggest risk. Did You know it was my heart all along? Don't let me hurt her, Lord. Make me the man she needs, because I'm pretty sure she's the woman I need.*

Gran came out on the porch to meet him, wrapping him in a fierce hug when he got out of the car. "I am so thankful y'all are safe and sound. What a gruesome business. I tell you, I'm sick and tired of people trying to take my loved ones down. We're due for some happy times out here. Overdue, if you ask me."

"Long overdue, Gran. And this episode's all but over, I think. But I'm with you—we need some smooth sailing for a change." He gave Gran his arm to lean on as they walked back up the porch steps. "How is she?"

Gran patted his arm. "Shaken, but strong. I like her." She looked at Witt. "You do, too."

He was too tired to fight Gran's legendary intuition. "Yeah, I do, but there's so much to…"

Gran stopped walking. "You stop right there. There is not 'so much' of anything. There's silly details that don't really matter, that only look big right now."

"We work together, Gran. That makes it complicated."

She gave him one of her looks. "Your grandfather and I worked together every single day of our lives. So did your father and his wife."

"And look what it did to them."

"Look what it did for Grandpa and I. I'm not proud of how Grayson treated you, but that's no reason you have to be unhappy. It's the saddest thing I know that neither of my boys saw the value in the family they had right in front of 'em. But you are not your father. I will not stand by and watch my grandson logic his way out of what could be the best thing to ever happen to him just because it's complicated." She began walking into the house without him, shaking her head. "Complicated. Why do my grandchildren make the simplest things in life all complicated?" At the door, she turned back to him. "Be a Buckton, child. Go get what's yours."

With that, she walked into the house, not seeming to care if he followed. He was so tired, he'd let her deliver that sermon without interrupting her to say he intended to do just what she'd said.

"I am, Gran," he defended himself to the empty yard. "That's why I'm here."

The screen door opened, and Jana walked out onto the porch, arms hugging her chest inside one of Ellie's knitted shawls that wrapped around her shoulders. "What?"

He ought to just charge up those steps, take her in his arms and declare all kinds of life-long love for her, but she looked fragile and tired. In need of tenderness, not grand, dramatic gestures. He skipped any attempt at explanation, walking closer to her instead. He waited for her arms to soften, for the protective clutch she held over herself to open up at his presence. It didn't. She'd been guarding herself for so long she didn't know how to stop. A surging need to protect her, to give her the security of his guardianship, welled up inside him.

Witt said the only thing that really mattered. "It's over. He can't hurt you anymore, Jana."

"I want to believe that."

He took a step closer to her. "You *can* believe that. He'll never hurt you because I won't let him."

Witt waited for the words to melt her rigid stance, but she still held herself tight. *Let me in, Jana. You can trust me not to hurt you.* "Jana…"

"He stole it, Witt. He took our night, the contest we were going to win, and he shot it to pieces."

"Ronnie did no such thing. He didn't take anything from us."

Her shoulders softened an almost imperceptible amount, her arms dropping just a little bit as she leaned against the porch post. "I wanted last night to be perfect."

He couldn't argue it had been perfect—it'd been the furthest thing from perfect. But… "We put an end to the fear that's been hanging over your head for years. That's something. That's good enough."

She shook her head. "Last night was supposed to be about the truck."

"And in spite of everything, we took second place, Jana. People voted for us even after we left and we took second place. Your cooking won us second place."

"There's no grant for second place."

"I don't need that grant. I told you that last night." He took another step closer, so that he was on the stair below her looking up into those impossibly brown eyes. "What I need to succeed is right here in front of me." Witt put his hands on her arms, grateful to feel her soften against his palms. "What I need to succeed, what I need *period*, is you."

"Witt…"

He pulled her toward him slowly, giving her the chance to lean in rather than forcing her even the slightest bit. "I know it feels like a huge risk. I'm terrified. Not because of all the reasons you think, but because I know this is all-or-nothing. You and me. I know you feel it. I know you've been hurt and I will not, *will not* hurt you.

"How can you be so sure?"

"Because this is worth everything to me. I thought the truck was the thing that secured my future, my life away from Star Beef, but it isn't. It's just a hunk of metal. That's the thing, Jana. Ronnie only hurt the truck. He meant to hurt us, but he can't. He can't touch us if we're together." He brought one hand up to her hair, practically swaying at the silky way it curled through his fingers. He wanted to bury his hands in that hair and kiss her until she had to cling to him to stay upright, but she deserved his caution. He had already decided he would stand here and open every corner of his heart to her until *she* kissed *him*, because the final crossing of this bridge between them was hers to make.

For once in his life, Witt Buckton was at a complete, vulnerable disadvantage, and didn't care. This was everything on the line, and he was not leaving this porch without her heart—because she already held his.

Chapter Seventeen

"Close your eyes," Jana said softly from her step above him on the porch.

Witt gave her one of his looks. "I am in no mood for a grilled cheese."

Rather than requesting again, Jana took one hand and brought it tenderly across his eyes, closing them. He begrudgingly complied, but slid his hands to her waist and kept them locked there. His hands, warm and large, said *I will not let you go* in a way his words could not.

She knew this was playful, childish even, but Jana also knew she needed this moment to gather herself. To look at this man and choose to entwine her future with his even more than it already was without falling into the magnetism of those astonishing blue eyes. Witt was right—this was all-or-nothing. There would be no casual, safe love between them.

Love. The word entered her mind with the ease of truth. She did love him. She loved his vibrancy, the way he held his ground, the way he gave in when he realized he was wrong. She loved his bold attack on life, the way he fought for his future even when life seemed ready to take it from him. She loved the way he trusted God but still dug in his heels and fought for himself and those he cared about. She glimpsed the woman she could be when she was with Witt. Ronnie's effect on her life had been to show her a hundred limitations, but Witt showed her a thousand possibilities. She wanted that. She wanted him. She wanted what she could be with him, and that was worth every risk.

Jana took his face in her hands, feeling his whole body come alive at her touch. It had been cruel to make him wait so long, standing there on the step below her with his eyes closed, but she'd wanted to be totally sure when she gave her heart to him.

The kiss was light, a tender promise, but all the more powerful for its stillness. His hands slid from holding her waist to wrapping his arms completely around her, and she

felt him breathe in and melt against her. Both
the times he'd held her in the past were in response to danger, but this was altogether different. This was an action, not a reaction. Her
body recognized its home in his arms, and the
sword of caution she'd been carrying for so
long finally fell from her hands. She kissed
him like the man he was, strong, deep, de-
clarative…and hers.

His hands slid up her back to bury themselves in her hair, and a moan of delight vi-
brated through his chest against her. "It does."

She pulled away for just a moment, only
able to bear the tiniest gap between them. "It
does what?"

"It feels like I thought it would. Actually,
better than I thought it would." Jana let her
head fall back a bit as the sensation of his
hands through her hair sent tingles all the
way to her toes. "Your hair has been driving
me mad since the day I met you."

"Kind of like your eyes," she replied, feeling the lightness of her smile everywhere.
"Those Buckton blue eyes."

"Legendary," he murmured against her
neck. "Like your grilled cheese."

"You're going to bring up food now?" She
laughed softly.

"I'm going to bring up food forever," he

said. Then he pulled back to look at her, and she felt those Buckton blues go through her, right down to the last careful corner of her heart. *"Forever."*

He was speaking of far more than grilled cheese, and she knew it. "Sounds delicious."

"I think we can make it, Jana."

"The sandwich?" she teased, giving herself the luxury of leaning into his embrace. Jana felt her eyes light up—a curious, sparkly sensation that had first started way back at the picnic across dueling cans of whipped cream. Now it had bloomed into affection. No, it had bloomed into love. A startling, unexpected love that was as delightfully joyful as it was deeply serious.

"That, too." Witt feathered one hand down her cheek, and Jana felt her knees go weak. It was okay to go weak right now because Witt was strong. They were stronger together than they were apart—if that wasn't reason to give their relationship a try, what was?

"I'm pretty sure I'm in love with you," he said, his voice soft and serious. Jana didn't think it was possible for his eyes to get any bluer than they already were, but they seemed to glow like the clearest of summer skies.

She put one hand on his chest, his heartbeat thrumming under her fingers. "Pretty sure?"

"Just a minute, I'll check." And with that he leaned in and kissed her again. *Exquisite* wasn't a strong enough word to describe the way he made her feel. "Yep," he said, his face flushed and his voice husky as he pulled away. "I'm a goner. Hopelessly in love with you."

Hopelessly? Witt's love gave her more hope than anything she'd felt in years. "Way far gone myself, actually," she admitted, amazed at how she fit perfectly in the circle of his arms.

"You're in love with me?" He looked half stunned, half as if he'd known it all along. She knew the dual sensation—loving Witt was both a huge surprise and the most natural thing in the whole world. She couldn't help but love him.

She nodded. "I am."

Witt laughed, then picked her up and swung her around. It was like some hokey scene from a movie, but she didn't care. Somehow the pile of challenges in front of them seemed smaller, easier now that they were really, truly together. "I am," Jana repeated as he deposited her back down on the porch. She may be standing on the Buckton front porch, but her feet weren't anywhere near touching the ground. "Now what?"

"Well," Witt replied, still grinning, "I was hoping for some breakfast. That thing the gas station called a burrito barely qualifies and I need some real food. Know anyone who can cook?"

"Come on inside," Jana invited, pulling him toward the door. "I think I can whip something up."

"No such thing," came Gran's voice from the other side of the screen. "I'm making pancakes."

Jana felt her cheeks go pink. Witt gave the old woman a mock glare. "How long have you been there?"

Gran winked. "Long enough, son. Long enough."

Gunner set his coffee down. "I assume Taylor's been charged?" The whole family had been gathered for breakfast and been brought up to speed. Well, on official business, anyway. The collection of amused looks Witt earned by not letting go of Jana's hand— except to eat, and barely even then—caught the family up on the day's other important developments.

"As the owner of the truck, I was able to press the property damage charges right then and there. The folks at the rodeo contest are talking about charging him with public endangerment if they can. They lost half their crowd after Ronnie's stunt."

"It was scary," Audie said. "I hope I never meet anybody that mean."

"I'm sorry you had to see that, sweetheart," Witt said as he watched Gunner put a protective arm around the girl. "You were especially brave." Witt hated what Ronnie had done to Jana, but he especially hated that the man was so cruel as to take his revenge in front of a whole crowd of innocent people. The idea of Audie and his own parents being witness to the truck's blood-red spatter made his stomach lurch.

"The truck will be all cleaned and repainted in a week. Insurance covered everything."

"But no restaurant grant," Jana added.

"I don't know about that," Ellie offered. "I was digging around my Restaurateurs Association contacts, and I found a small-business program you can apply for. It's not as much—not enough to fund a restaurant—but it might be enough to add another truck, maybe two."

"Not quite your speedy timetable, but expansion just the same," Gunner said.

Witt looked at Jana. "Maybe a slower pace is just what we need."

"What have you done to that man?" Ellie asked, clearly amused.

"Well, isn't it obvious?" Gran said.

"Am I supposed to understand this?" Audie asked, propping her small elbows up on the table.

The whole family laughed, making baby Trey squeal from his high chair. "In about ten years or so," Audie's mother said.

"Fifteen. Twenty, even," Gunner revised, sending everyone into more laughter. It made Witt sorry for whatever boy chose to date Audie. Little Audie may be Gunner's stepdaughter, but no father was ever more attentive or protective. Witt looked around the table, from Gran to Gunner to Brooke to Ellie and finally to Jana. There was a table in San Antonio filled with other blood relatives, but around this table he'd discovered the family of his heart.

"I have some other good news to share," Ellie said.

"You eloped?" Gunner teased.

"Oh no, you're not getting out of hosting a wedding so easy. New Year's Eve I am going to marry that sheriff and nothing is going to stop me. I like parties too much, and I've waited too long to shrug this one off. No, my news is that Luke and Tess might actually come home for the wedding."

"Well, I figured Tess would make it here," Gunner replied. "But Luke?" Witt knew the whole family would be pleased about Gunner's younger twin siblings' return to Blue Thorn Ranch for the event. The only sad thing about Gunner's wedding was the fact that the twins hadn't come. Those two had been gone for years.

"That's one of the reasons I chose New Year's Eve," Ellie went on, "Luke's got just enough time in between events to show up."

"Rodeo star," Witt offered to Jana by way of explanation. "Very famous, very busy."

"Very convinced of his own importance," Ellie replied. "Let's just say I encouraged him to rethink his priorities."

"Meaning you threatened him," Gunner added.

"I might have reminded him that I could arrange a conversation between his manager and Gran." Ellie's smirk was a victorious as it was devious.

"Never tangle with cousin Ellie," Witt warned.

"Never tangle with a bride about her wedding day," Ellie corrected.

Gran's eyes glistened with happy tears. "My grandchildren back on the Blue Thorn. I've been asking the Good Lord for that gift for years." She reached over and gave baby Trey a tender kiss on his forehead. "And great-grandbabies. My stars, but I am a blessed woman." She shifted and kissed Audie. "All my great-grandchildren make me happy."

Breakfast carried on like a party after that, all noise and happiness and food. The joy of it all seeped in as the perfect antidote to all of yesterday's stress and strain. But a ranch never stopped—for crisis or joy—and soon enough the family went their ways to take care of chores. Witt and Jana stayed behind to take care of the dishes.

"What if Luke or Tess come home for good?" Jana ventured with a sideways glance at Witt as he stood beside her at the sink. "How would you feel about that?"

"Not much chance of that happening, I think," he replied. "Should I feel something in particular?" He had an idea where this was going, but wanted to see how Jana would bring up the tender subject.

"Well," she replied carefully, "I just wondered if you might be worried all those full-blooded Bucktons might eventually squeeze you out of the business. I mean, I think you have a fair reason to be touchy on the subject."

"I'm a full-blooded Buckton, too, you know," he teased. Some part of him liked that she'd considered how Luke's and Tess's possible return might affect him.

She flicked a dollop of soap suds in his direction. "You know what I mean."

He moved closer to her, so that their arms touched. "I do. And thanks for considering that." He pushed out a breath. "I admit, there was a short flash of panic when Ellie told me, but it's not the same here." Witt searched for a way to explain a difference he barely understood himself. "This side of the family is different. Nobody's battling for a place in line here—there's room for everybody without having to push anyone out." *There's even room for you,* he added silently, unsure if it was safe to say. Everything felt too new and fragile between him and Jana just now. Wonderful, but delicate.

"I watched how she went out of her way to declare Audie as one of her great-grandchildren," Jana said, handing Witt the big crockery mixing bowl that had held the batter.

"That's Gran. That woman has space in her heart for everybody. She's done the same for me."

Jana stopped washing and looked at him. "Do you feel that unwelcome with your own family?"

Unwelcome. That came close to hitting the nail on the head, especially now. The chance of repairing his relationship with Mom and Dad had been another casualty of last night's chaos. He'd found them and checked on them, but the interaction had gone badly. Dad behaved as if Witt had somehow put them in danger on purpose. He'd allowed himself a fragile hope that their appearance was the start of reconciliation, but the whole two-minute conversation as they were rushing to their car had been sour and cold and just made everything worse between them. "Mary and I were close before she married Cole," he offered, "and I think we'll get over this rough spot eventually. It's just that, well, there's being loved for who you ought to be, and then there's being loved for who you are." He rinsed the soap off the big bowl and set it in the drying rack. "I know faith is a part of that, but I think it's as much who Gran is. Believe me, Gunner's dad was no saint in the fatherhood department, either." He leaned against the counter for a moment. "I think things might have been different if my dad hadn't moved away."

Jana looked up at him, eyes soft with compassion and affection. "But you got to come back and be near all this love. I see why you did. I'm glad I get to be near, too."

Witt held her gaze, feeling like he had come home in more ways than one. "There's so much love here. Love and faith and strength, you know? It seeps into you. Do you feel it?"

"All over," she said. "Thank you." Now it was her eyes that glistened.

"For what?"

"For bringing me into this. For making me feel safe. For…" She was deciding whether to say *love* out loud here in the kitchen where they could be overheard. Speaking *love* aloud ought to be the easiest thing in the world—especially in this house—but it was scary, too.

He leaned in and kissed her forehead. "Me, too."

Her eyes glowed, and then without hesitation, she wrapped her hands around his neck and gave him a kiss that set off rockets in his chest. Soapy water dripped down the back of his shirt and he couldn't have cared less.

A set of high-pitched giggles broke off the moment, and Witt turned to see Audie standing in the doorway. "Everybody's always kissing in this house," she proclaimed with an eye roll.

With that, Witt dashed across the kitchen floor, hands still wet, and snagged a squealing Audie up off the floor to plant a great big noisy kiss on her cheek. "That tickles!" She giggled. "Stop it, cousin Witt!" she called through peals of laughter, squirming as he made raspberries into her neck.

"Never, cousin Audie!" he teased, making her laugh even more. He really did feel a special affinity for the girl. He felt a special affinity for everything about the Blue Thorn Ranch. Star Beef was the home of his lineage, but the Blue Star was the home of his heart.

And since his heart now belonged to Jana, that made it her home, too.

Chapter Eighteen

It was more than just pushing open the counter flap doors on the Blue Thorn truck. Jana felt as if she were declaring the relaunch of her life. Now that the shadow that had hung over her was gone, Jana discovered she loved the bright colors of the truck as a sign of the bright colors she felt in her life. Blue skies and sunshine. She'd never been more ready to get cooking.

Spatula Dave had made good on his word. In fact, they had gained so much notoriety from his published recant and the terrible incident at the rodeo that business looked like it would be booming.

"I wonder if your stalker dude knows how much of a favor he did us," Jose mused as he lined up the condiment bottles in their places. Jose had taken to calling Ronnie "your stalker dude." While crude, the off-color yet silly nickname just helped Jana put the whole thing behind her where it belonged.

"If you think that means I'll thank him— ever—you're wrong."

"No, man, I'd want to slug him if they gave me the chance, same as you."

Jana found it amusing that Jose thought her strong enough to land a punch on the likes of Ronnie. For all his unusual wisdom, Jose was still a kid with a kid's idea of what constituted correct behavior. "I don't want to slug Ronnie." When he raised a dark eyebrow, she added, "Mostly. I want him to pay for what he did, but I don't really see that in terms of a well-landed punch."

"I don't know," Jose offered as he pulled tomatoes from the box under the counter. "You look like you could pack a good one to me."

Jana gave him a quizzical look. "Thanks, I think. But no thanks on beating up Ronnie."

"Thing is," Jose continued as he dumped the tomatoes into the colander and began washing them, "he did the exact opposite of what he wanted, you know? I mean look at us." Jose shut off the water and nodded toward the electronic tablet in its holder on the wall. "We got more *Azulos* than ever— we doubled our followers in the last week."

He pulled up the truck's social media page, grinning as he pointed to the number that tabulated followers. "If this keeps up, by tomorrow we'll have more than the guys who won first place."

Jana had to admit, that was an impressive outcome. "Okay, I'll admit, that's a good thing. And don't think I don't recognize how much of that is your doing. You're as good at publicity as you are at cooking."

"You're different, too, Chef. Stalker dude didn't win there, either."

She almost didn't want to ask. "How so?"

"You don't look over your shoulder anymore. I could never figure out what it was that I saw—that sort of nervous thing that made you quick to bite, you know? Only it's gone now. Things are different." He waggled one eyebrow at her. "Especially between you and boss. He's been into you from the beginning, and I was pretty sure you were into him, too. I was wondering how long it would take you two to figure it out." He said the last part as if he was glad he didn't have to step in and play matchmaker. Jana couldn't come up with a reply for that, especially with the "you crazy kids" look in his eye.

Jana turned on the grill. "You've got a ways

to go with your cooking skills, but your chef's personality is all set."

"Witt's going to help me with those applications to cooking schools." The bravado faded a bit, a true hint as to how daunting the boy found the prospect of truly getting serious about cooking. He'd never said, but Jana suspected Jose would be the first in his family to even consider college. It felt good to give a talented kid a leg up toward such a bright future. Especially a kid she liked as much as Jose.

"He ought to. You deserve to go." As she pulled the meat from the refrigerator, she added, "I'll be sorry to lose you, but thrilled to see you work toward your own career. Maybe in the second Blue Thorn truck, when we're ready."

"I'm ready now," he boasted, grinning.

"No, you're not," she countered. "But I have no doubt you will be."

Chapter Nineteen

Witt halted the car at the entrance of the Star Ranch. He'd been mostly silent the entire hour-and-a-half ride from Austin to his family's home north of San Antonio. "This was a bad idea."

Jana grabbed his hand. "No, it's a good idea. It's Christmas, Witt. You should be with your family. It will just be hard at first."

He ran his free hand through his hair. "The last time I walked out this gate, I was an angry ball of bitterness. Feels weird to be back here. Wrong." He looked at Jana. "This could get ugly. I shouldn't have made you come with me."

"This from the guy who held me while my ex lobbed paint balls at our truck. Even if this does get ugly—which it might not—we still wouldn't be nearly even. Ugh," she added, shaking off a shudder. "I don't even want to dignify Ronnie by calling him my ex. We were over so long ago." She squeezed Witt's hand. "My life is all about what's ahead of me now. You should have that, too."

He squeezed right back. "I do have that."

Jana took his hand in both of hers. "Not really. Take it from someone who knows— you'll have this hanging over your head until you make peace with it. This is your family, Witt. You've got to at least try."

"Pray. Hard," he said shakily.

Jana brought his hand up to her lips and kissed it. "What do you think I've been doing the whole drive?"

Witt nodded. Then he took a deep breath, and pressed the button at the ranch entrance.

"Can't you just go on in?"

"I could," Witt replied, "but somehow I don't feel as if I ought to. Like I said, the last time I went through this gate things were an angry mess. I actually wasn't sure I'd ever come back."

Jana wondered how a gulf so large could spread between people who were supposed to love each other—but then Ronnie had already shown her how sour relationships could go, hadn't he? "It's worth it to try," she repeated. She felt so much lighter, so much more at peace with the world now, and wanted that same peace for Witt.

"Witt, honey, is that you?" came an older woman's voice over the intercom.

Witt's entire face registered his recognition at the voice. "Yeah, Mom, it's me." Whatever distance had spread between Witt and his father, it was clear it hadn't truly pushed Witt away from his mother. Jana's throat tightened at the emotion she saw in Witt's eyes. He loved his family, and wanted nothing more than to feel their love for him. Her mama had adored Witt from the moment they met. But if Jana was honest, she was more than a bit apprehensive about meeting Witt's parents.

"Come on up, son. I'm so glad you're here."

The driveway up to the main house at the Star Ranch was similar to the one at the Blue Thorn, only larger and far more impressive. Whereas the Blue Thorn was warm and welcoming and a little worn around the edges, the Star was big and bold and powerful—but somewhat cold. Decked out for the holidays like a movie set, all sparkling and dramatic yet lacking in the warmth that would make it feel like a real home rather than a facade. "Wow," Jana said, a bit stunned.

"Yep. The Star is nothing if not impressive." Jana could feel Witt's tension as he parked the car; she felt tense herself. This place spoke of success—the achievement of it, and the expectation of it. She could see why Witt always said the Blue Thorn was more home to him than the ranch where he was raised. Jana had taken extra care to dress nicely, but already she felt out of her league. The garage alone looked bigger than Mama's house. Everything gleamed.

A graceful, beautifully dressed woman walked out on the porch. Slender as a willow, she bore the casual air of someone who no longer needs to try to impress. She looked very much like Witt, but with hazel eyes—the Buckton blues clearly coming from Witt's father.

By the time Witt had gotten out of the car and come around to open Jana's door, Witt's mother had reached the two of them. There was an awkward, hesitant moment where no one seemed to know what greeting to use, but then the woman pulled her son into a fierce hug, squeezing so tight Jana felt tears sting her eyes.

"Witt, my boy," Mrs. Buckton said, her own voice breaking. "You're here."

She pulled away after a moment, gathering herself back into the elegant woman Jana had first seen. She extended a slim, graceful hand adorned with stunning silver-and-turquoise jewelry. "You must be Jana."

"Hello, Mrs. Buckton," Jana said, telling herself not to be intimidated. Her hair must look like a pile of tangles next to Marjorie Buckton's sleek salt-and-pepper bob.

"Call me Marjorie, my dear. It's lovely to meet you. Merry Christmas. Mary has told me a lot about you and the amazing things you do with Gunner's meat."

Jana noticed she referred to the Blue Thorn product, Witt's professional stock and trade, as "Gunner's meat." From the way she felt Witt's reaction, he'd noticed, as well. *Grace, Lord*, she prayed. *Send us grace. All You can spare.*

"Come on in, you two. Mary and Cole should be here in ten minutes or so."

Jana watched Witt pull in a breath to ask the question that had hung heavily in the air since they'd stepped onto Star land.

"Your father's out with the herd at the moment," Marjorie said before he could even get the words out. "But he'll be in for supper." Not here to greet his son's long-awaited return to the ranch? Jana couldn't decide if that was cruelty or grace. Based on Witt's expression, he couldn't decide, either. Maybe it was best for Witt to make his peace with his mother first, working his way up to Cole and Mary and finally Grayson. *So much hard healing to be done. I'm trusting You know what's best here, Lord.*

Marjorie took Jana's elbow. "What a scare we all had at the rodeo. Dreadful thing. Is everything okay now?" Her words were warm, as if she truly regretted what a mess all of it turned out to be. Jana believed her to be sincere. After all, what mother wants her son estranged or in harm's way?

"I'd like to think that's all behind me—and the truck—now. Witt was amazing during all that. I don't know how I would have coped if he hadn't been there protecting me." It felt a bit cheesy to put it that way, but Jana wanted Marjorie to know how wonderful her son had been to her.

"That doesn't surprise me one bit," Marjorie replied. "Witt's a good man."

Witt reached back for Jana's hand. "So this," he said, gesturing around the ranch with his other hand, "is where I grew up. What do you think?"

Jana wasn't quite sure how to answer that. The whole place felt so different from the Witt she knew, and with his mother standing right there trying not to look at their joined hands, everything felt awkward and forced.

"It's beautiful," she ventured, for the land really was spectacular. The house was large and elegant. Showy, but not in an entirely bad way. This branch of the Bucktons had clearly seen much more prosperity than Gunner's side—and that didn't make them bad.

Witt's stiff walk and the vise grip he had on Jana's hand? That spoke of other things. He was a different person here—hard-shelled and defensive. The warm confidence that drew her to him seemed hidden under a cold armor.

"Life's been very good to us," Marjorie offered. "Star Beef has become one of the largest cattle operations in the county."

"Cole and Dad make an unstoppable team." Witt's words had just a hint of an edge to them. Jana saw Marjorie's face pinch a bit at the tone.

"So, it seems, do the two of you. Mary tells me you took second place even though that horrid business took you out of the event hours before it ended." Marjorie turned to Jana. "I do hope I can convince you to share your coleslaw recipe with me. Mary raved about it."

So Mary had been singing Blue Thorn Burgers's praises to Witt's mom and dad. Jana chose to view that as evidence that

Mary wanted to patch things up. Maybe the three women in this struggle could convince the three men to call a truce. It might take a while, but today was at least a first step.

"Supper wasn't *so* awful, was it?" Mary walked toward the barn beside Witt while Jana exchanged recipes in the kitchen with Mom. Cole and Dad had been coolly polite, holing themselves up in his father's study almost immediately after the meal. Witt had very pointedly not been invited. It didn't sting as much as it would have a year ago.

"I wasn't expecting warm fuzzies, Mary," Witt admitted. He let out a resigned breath. "We ate in the same room and didn't yell at each other." He looked at his sister. "I wasn't sure we'd even get that far."

"Well, you're the one who left," Mary replied a bit sharply.

"Did you expect me to stay?" Witt challenged. "Did you think I could just smile and be happy with how things worked out?" He refused to believe Mary was oblivious to the king-size snub his father had pulled off, not just bringing Cole into the fold but approving his five-year plan that showed Witt's role considerably diminished. She had to understand why he'd left. Then again, he'd never explained it to her—never even thought he'd needed to explain.

"Well, no, not before." She sat down on a low bench just outside the barn. "But things are different now, aren't they?"

"Only because I've changed. Dad hasn't. Cole hasn't."

Mary crossed her arms over her chest. "Cole doesn't have anything against you, Witt. He never has."

Witt stood in front of her, feeing his defenses spring up despite every effort not to get riled. "You ought to know me well enough to see I'm not the kind to stand in line behind your husband in my own family's business."

"Why do you act like Cole set out to steal something from you? Why can't he just be a welcome addition to our family?"

Witt stared at his sister. "You even have to ask? Don't you understand the difference between an addition and a replacement? Him coming in meant that I was pushed out."

"You never behaved like you wanted this business." She gestured around them. "You always acted like none of this mattered to you. You did the work and you were good at it, but it never seemed to make you happy." It wasn't the work that had made him unhappy but rather the fact that it had never seemed to be good enough for his father—but he didn't want to get into that argument again.

"Cole loves this land, loves what we do," Mary added. "Why do you hate Dad for welcoming that?"

"I never hated this place." He turned from Mary to look over the pastures, surprised by the warring emotions of loyalty and betrayal that had seemed to choke him from the moment Mom had hugged him. "I hated what it did to me." The truth that stunned him even as he spoke the words. "I hated the way I was never enough. And then I hated the way Cole was just *so* perfect." After a moment, he dared himself to speak the real truth. "I hated the way Dad looked like he'd been waiting for Cole his whole life because I wasn't whatever it was I was supposed to be."

There was a long silence. Then Witt heard Mary stand up and come to stand beside him. He still couldn't bring himself to look at her, but she took his hand. The gesture brought a lump to his throat. "You can't blame Cole for that. Dad made this problem, I get that. But I wish you wouldn't blame the man I love for loving what means most to me."

Witt squeezed her hand, lost for words.

"I miss you," she said, tears in her voice. "We all do."

"Even Dad?" Witt had to ask.

"Even Dad. I think he knows he pushed you away. He just doesn't know how to pull you back. Or even if he can."

"He could at least try."

Mary pulled on Witt's hand until he turned to her. "Believe it or not, I think he was trying today. Were you?"

"I don't know. I'm here, aren't I?"

"It's going to take a bit more than just standing in the same room without locking horns."

Witt sighed. "That's exactly what Jana said."

Mary wiped her eyes. "Well, she's right."

Witt watched his sister walk over to a stone container near the bench and pull a sprig of pine from inside. The house was beautiful at the holidays, always had been. *Loving what means most to me*, Mary had said. He loved the Blue Thorn truck and all it stood for far more than he felt any affinity to the upscale enterprise that Star Beef was. That wasn't wrong or disloyal—it just was. "He'll always see me as the deserter."

"Not if you come home every once in a while." She twirled the pine branch between two fingers. "Invite him and mom to visit the truck again."

Witt laughed. "After the rodeo? He'd never."

"He might. And if he resisted, you know Mom would drag him anyway." She handed the branch to Witt. "You belong there. It's made you happy—even I can see it. Why don't you show Dad that for yourself?"

"He doesn't want to see it."

"No, he doesn't—so don't give him a choice. Blue Thorn Burgers is catering cousin Ellie's rehearsal dinner next week, aren't they?"

It was to be Jose's first true test of working the truck on his own. "So?"

"So Dad and Mom will be there. Cole and I will be there. How about you serve burgers with a side of olive branch?"

"That's a terrible joke," Witt offered. "But it's probably a good idea."

Mary pulled him into a hug, and he didn't resist. He'd missed her more than he'd realized until just this moment. "Not probably," she said. "It is a good idea. One I'll hold you to, brother. What I want for Christmas is to put an end to all this division, and I think you can do that."

Witt wasn't sure he could make good on

that promise, but for the first time since he'd stormed off this ranch, he felt that with Jana at his side he might be ready to try.

Chapter Twenty

The Blue Thorn Ranch was buzzing with the festivities of Ellie and Nash's wedding. Ellie loved projects, and she'd poured her heart and soul into this event. It showed everywhere. Jana admired the decorations that had turned the barn into a festive hall, right down to thoughtful touches like place cards tied with tiny turquoise bandanna ribbons. Jana's whole heart seemed to fill with the bursting emotions of the day.

"You okay?" Witt said, returning from his search for yet more tissues. "I hadn't pegged you for the kind to cry at weddings."

She was embarrassed at how Ellie and Nash's vows and now their first dance had choked her up, but Witt seemed oddly charmed by it. He'd even kissed one or two tears away, which of course only choked her up more. "They're so happy, aren't they?" she offered, as if that explained the waterworks.

"Kind of nice to see." Witt wrapped an arm around her. He'd been the perfect, attentive date today, while he'd been the perfect business partner last night for the rehearsal dinner—watching over Jose and how he fed the guests but still making sure he and Jana got to step back and enjoy themselves as guests. "The whole thing has been a perfect happy ending. Even Tess and Luke showed up. It's good to be reminded that God still makes happy endings in the world."

She cast her gaze up into those amazing Buckton blues, her heart doing what felt like the hundredth flip of the day. Today marked the first time she'd seen Witt in a suit, and the smart tan jacket and brilliant blue tie set his eyes off like beacons. If there'd been any question she was head over heels in love with Witt Buckton, today sealed her heart's fate. *I want this for us,* she dared to pray. *I love this man and this family.* "It sure is," she agreed.

Further proof of that arrived with Grayson and Marjorie Buckton, who walked up to greet Witt and Jana. "More food," Marjorie happily groaned as they looked toward the bursting banquet tables set up across the front lawn. "After last night I thought I wouldn't need to eat for a week."

"The dinner was good," Grayson agreed. Jana had been pleased Grayson had offered one or two hesitant compliments last night. Witt and his father weren't cozy just yet, but they had managed to build on the prickly bridge strung between them at Christmas. And not just he and his son; one of her favorite moments from last night had been Gran's open, grateful tears when Grayson had stepped back onto Blue Thorn land for the first time in decades.

"You look lovely, dear," Marjorie said.

"Thank you," Jana replied, smiling. Marjorie, of course, looked stunning, perfectly dressed in a peach linen dress that made her silver hair glow.

"Hey, bosses!" Jose swaggered by and waved, raising a "check me out" eyebrow at his date and dashing outfit. He'd been a hit last night, and knew it. She couldn't fault the boy for his boasting today—he reigned as king over the boisterous band of teens who'd been invited to the wedding. Ellie and Nash were on the second session of the after-school program they ran at Martins Gap Community Church, where today's ceremony had taken place.

Witt grabbed Jose's elbow as he strutted by. "Where on earth did you find confetti cannons?"

The "Car Guys" and the "Yarn Gals"—for Nash taught car repair and Ellie taught knitting—had somehow procured a pair of confetti cannons and set them off as Nash and Ellie exited the church. The stunt had doused the happy couple and every guest in a blue-and-yellow blizzard that had been as amusing as it was extreme.

"Internet, amigo. We all chipped in. Couldn't just get those two a toaster, now, could we?"

"I'll be picking confetti out of my hair for a week," Jana teased. In fact, Witt had seemed to rather enjoy running his hands through her hair every few minutes under the pretense of finding "one more bit." She caught Jose's eye. "You did great last night, Jose. Austin Culinary should be glad to get you."

Jose gave a cocky wink and a big thumbs-up. "*Sí,* Chef."

"Born charmer, that boy." Jana laughed affectionately. She'd come to adore Jose, healthy ego and all. Witt had helped him finish his application just last week. Even Ellie had managed to find time away from wedding preparations to have her old boss from her Atlanta restaurant chain send a letter of recommendation. It made Jana's heart glow to think of Jose's bright future. Her heart glowed at her own bright future, too.

She felt Witt tug at her hand. "Come on. There's something I want to show you. Before Mark and his band start up and there's no quiet spot left on the ranch, that is."

He'd already shown her all his favorite spots on the ranch. Jana couldn't imagine what would pull Witt away from the festivities this afternoon. With the success of the burgers last night, the two of them had been fielding compliments all day, and Witt rarely turned away from praise like that.

She gave him a questioning look when he stopped in an ordinary corner of the horse barn. No lovely view greeted her, no family possession, just a rustic wooden wall and a collection of well-used implements.

"Yeah, I know," he conceded. "Nothing much to look at. But here—" he gestured around, eyes bright "—here is where Blue Thorn Burgers was born. Ellie and I were talking after things went sour at Cole's arrival."

"Okay," she replied, still not quite sure where this was heading.

"She knew I wanted to disappear like Gunner had. To just take off, to show the world I didn't need Star Beef or even family. I might have, too, if she hadn't floated the idea of bringing me in to run Blue Thorn Burgers. Gunner was already thinking in terms of the retail store here in Martins Gap, but I had the idea of the truck." His face took on the spark of success that it always did when he talked about the truck—or *trucks*, for he'd started speaking in plurals now and she knew he saw the future in terms as bright as she felt.

She looked around, feeling his gratitude for what had begun in these meager surroundings. "So this is the birthplace of your empire, hmm?"

Witt wrapped his hand around hers. "More than that. I think of this place as the start of my whole new life. My real life. The one that's mine." His other hand wrapped around her waist and pulled her close. "The one that's *ours*."

Jana felt the thrill his eyes could always produce under her skin. The man was a force of nature, a source of power, a man whose combination of faith and determination made her feel as if anything was possible. How differently, how splendidly her future seemed to spread before her now. "I think I like this barn," she teased, touching a corner of the rough wood with Witt's sense of reverence for it.

"I think I like this life," Witt replied. "Actually, I don't think, I know. I love this life. I love what's ahead." One hand rose up to stroke her cheek, and Jana felt the world swirl around her. "I love you. I love your food. I love your energy. I love the way God shows me the best parts of myself through you. I want God to show you the best parts of yourself through me."

"He has." The words came out as an astonished breath, an exhalation of awe. It was true—this place was the furthest thing from ordinary. Here, looking into Witt's eyes, it felt like a sacred space.

"I never want that to stop. I want to spend my life with you. Marry me, Jana Powers. Let's spend the rest of our lives cooking up the best possible future—the one God has in store."

He was asking her to marry him. The world around them seemed to fill with brightness and possibility as she embraced the thought. She would never struggle alone again. The thing she'd prayed for, the thing she knew

Mama had prayed for every day, had been laid in front of her at this very moment. Not a single shred of hesitation filled her heart when she said, "Yes."

Witt's smile was miles beyond warm. "That's what your mom said, too."

She laughed, feeling light and sparkly. "You asked?"

"You weren't the only one who called your mom on Christmas Day. She also said, 'What took you so long?'" A warm laugh rumbled through Witt's chest as he held her tight. "So I decided I couldn't wait, even though I like Nash too much to steal his thunder today. We'll have to keep this between us for now, but after watching Nash and Ellie I couldn't wait a moment longer." He kissed her left hand. "The ring is still back in Austin. Will you forgive me for jumping the gun?"

"You've never been the patient sort. I love that about you. I love you."

He kissed her, slowly and tenderly as if they had all the time in the world. And after all, didn't they? "Talk to me about food forever. Make me grilled cheese for the rest of my life."

"With pleasure," Jana said softly before she kissed him back to let him know how much she liked that idea. A true partner was a wonderful thing. But a loving husband in the new year? Well, that was a recipe for perfect happiness.

* * * * *

Don't miss these other BLUE THORN RANCH *stories from Allie Pleiter:*

THE TEXAS RANCHER'S RETURN
COMING HOME TO TEXAS

Find more great reads at
www.LoveInspired.com

Dear Reader,

Jana introduced herself to me one morning with no warning—and now that I know her better, it doesn't surprise me. God often brings people into our lives who surprise us. The challenge is to remember that God brings them into our lives for a purpose, even when we struggle to see it. I expect Jana would say the same about Witt. That's what makes their romance all the more sweet—it's that wonderful, slow transition from bafflement to affection. Those are my favorite books, and I hope they are yours, as well.

You'll be delighted to know that Luke does indeed come home—but you'll have to wait for the next book to find out how and why.

I always love to hear from readers. You can reach me via email at allie@alliepleiter. com, at my website www.alliepleiter.com, by post at PO Box 7026 Villa Park, IL 60181, or through Facebook and Twitter.

Blessings,

Allie Pleiter

LARGER-PRINT BOOKS!

GET 2 FREE LARGER-PRINT NOVELS PLUS 2 FREE MYSTERY GIFTS

Love Inspired ®

SUSPENSE

RIVETING INSPIRATIONAL ROMANCE

Larger-print novels are now available...

REQUEST YOUR FREE BOOKS!
2 FREE WHOLESOME ROMANCE NOVELS IN LARGER PRINT
PLUS 2 FREE MYSTERY GIFTS

❋❋❋❋❋❋❋❋❋❋❋❋❋❋❋❋❋❋❋❋

HEARTWARMING™

❅❅❅❅❅❅❅❅❅❅❅❅❅❅❅❅❅❅❅❅

Wholesome, tender romances

YES! Please send me 2 FREE Harlequin® Heartwarming Larger-Print novels and my 2 FREE mystery gifts (gifts worth about $10). After receiving them, if I don't wish to receive any more books, I can return the shipping statement marked "cancel." If I don't cancel, I will receive 4 brand-new larger-print novels every month and be billed just $5.24 per book in the U.S. or $5.99 per book in Canada. That's a savings of at least 19% off the cover price. It's quite a bargain! Shipping and handling is just 50¢ per book in the U.S. and 75¢ per book in Canada.* I understand that accepting the 2 free books and gifts places me under no obligation to buy anything. I can always return a shipment and cancel at any time. Even if I never buy another book, the two free books and gifts are mine to keep forever.

161/361 IDN GHX2

Name   (PLEASE PRINT)

Address   Apt. #

City   State/Prov.   Zip/Postal Code

Signature (if under 18, a parent or guardian must sign)

Mail to the **Reader Service:**
IN U.S.A.: P.O. Box 1867, Buffalo, NY 14240-1867
IN CANADA: P.O. Box 609, Fort Erie, Ontario L2A 5X3

* Terms and prices subject to change without notice. Prices do not include applicable taxes. Sales tax applicable in N.Y. Canadian residents will be charged applicable taxes. Offer not valid in Quebec. This offer is limited to one order per household. Not valid for current subscribers to Harlequin Heartwarming larger-print books. All orders subject to credit approval. Credit or debit balances in a customer's account(s) may be offset by any other outstanding balance owed by or to the customer. Please allow 4 to 6 weeks for delivery. Offer available while quantities last.

Your Privacy—The Reader Service is committed to protecting your privacy. Our Privacy Policy is available online at www.ReaderService.com or upon request from the Reader Service.

We make a portion of our mailing list available to reputable third parties that offer products we believe may interest you. If you prefer that we not exchange your name with third parties, or if you wish to clarify or modify your communication preferences, please visit us at www.ReaderService.com/consumerchoice or write to us at Reader Service Preference Service, P.O. Box 9062, Buffalo, NY 14240-9062. Include your complete name and address.

HW15

WESTERN WP PROMISES

YES! Please send me **The Western Promises Collection** in Larger Print. This collection begins with 3 FREE books and 2 FREE gifts (gifts valued at approx. $14.00 retail) in the first shipment, along with the other first 4 books from the collection! If I do not cancel, I will receive 8 monthly shipments until I have the entire 51-book Western Promises collection. I will receive 2 or 3 FREE books in each shipment and I will pay just $4.99 US/ $5.89 CDN for each of the other four books in each shipment, plus $2.99 for shipping and handling per shipment. *If I decide to keep the entire collection, I'll have paid for only 32 books, because 19 books are FREE! I understand that accepting the 3 free books and gifts places me under no obligation to buy anything. I can always return a shipment and cancel at any time. My free books and gifts are mine to keep no matter what I decide.

272 HCN 3070 472 HCN 3070

Name	(PLEASE PRINT)	
Address		Apt. #
City	State/Prov.	Zip/Postal Code

Signature (if under 18, a parent or guardian must sign)

Mail to the **Reader Service:**

IN U.S.A.: P.O. Box 1867, Buffalo, NY 14240-1867
IN CANADA: P.O. Box 609, Fort Erie, Ontario L2A 5X3

LARGER-PRINT BOOKS!

GET 2 FREE
LARGER-PRINT NOVELS
PLUS 2 FREE
MYSTERY GIFTS

Love Inspired®

Larger-print novels are now available...

LILP15